UNDER THE REDWOODS

BRET HARTE

1ST WORLD
LIBRARY
Literary Society

Under the Redwoods

Bret Harte

© 1st World Library, 2008
PO Box 2211
Fairfield, IA 52556
www.1stworldlibrary.com
First Edition

LCCN: 2007935365

Softcover ISBN: 978-1-4218-9318-1
Hardcover ISBN: 978-1-4218-9418-8
eBook ISBN: 978-1-4218-9218-4

Purchase *"Under the Redwoods"*
as a traditional bound book at:
www.1stWorldLibrary.com/purchase.asp?ISBN=978-1-4218-9318-1

1st World Library is a literary, educational organization
dedicated to:

- Creating a free internet library of downloadable ebooks

- Hosting writing competitions and offering book publishing
scholarships.

Interested in more 1st World Library books? contact:
literacy@1stworldlibrary.com
Check us out at: www.1stworldlibrary.com

1ˢᵗ World Library Literary Society

Giving Back to the World

"If you want to work on the core problem, it's early school literacy."

- James Barksdale, former CEO of Netscape

"No skill is more crucial to the future of a child, or to a democratic and prosperous society, than literacy."

- Los Angeles Times

"Literacy... means far more than learning how to read and write... The aim is to transmit... knowledge and promote social participation."

- UNESCO

"Literacy is not a luxury, it is a right and a responsibility. If our world is to meet the challenges of the twenty-first century we must harness the energy and creativity of all our citizens."

- President Bill Clinton

"Parents should be encouraged to read to their children, and teachers should be equipped with all available techniques for teaching literacy, so the varying needs and capacities of individual kids can be taken into account."

- Hugh Mackay

CONTENTS

JIMMY'S BIG BROTHER FROM CALIFORNIA

As night crept up from the valley that stormy afternoon, Sawyer's Ledge was at first quite blotted out by wind and rain, but presently reappeared in little nebulous star-like points along the mountain side, as the straggling cabins of the settlement were one by one lit up by the miners returning from tunnel and claim. These stars were of varying brilliancy that evening, two notably so—one that eventually resolved itself into a many-candled illumination of a cabin of evident festivity; the other into a glimmering taper in the window of a silent one. They might have represented the extreme mutations of fortune in the settlement that night: the celebration of a strike by Robert Falloner, a lucky miner; and the sick-bed of Dick Lasham, an unlucky one.

The latter was, however, not quite alone. He was ministered to by Daddy Folsom, a weak but emotional and aggressively hopeful neighbor, who was sitting beside the wooden bunk whereon the invalid lay. Yet there was something perfunc-tory in his attitude: his eyes were continually straying to the window, whence the illuminated Falloner festivities could be seen between the trees, and his ears were more intent on the songs and laughter that came faintly from the distance than on the feverish breathing and unintelligible moans of the sufferer.

Nevertheless he looked troubled equally by the condition of his charge and by his own enforced absence from the revels. A more impatient moan from the sick man, however, brought a change to his abstracted face, and he turned to him with an exaggerated expression of sympathy.

"In course! Lordy! I know jest what those pains are: kinder ez ef you was havin' a tooth pulled that had roots branchin' all over ye! My! I've jest had 'em so bad I couldn't keep from yellin'! That's hot rheumatics! Yes, sir, I oughter know! And" (confidentially) "the sing'ler thing about 'em is that they get worse jest as they're going off—sorter wringin' yer hand and punchin' ye in the back to say 'Good-by.' There!" he continued, as the man sank exhaustedly back on his rude pillow of flour-sacks. "There! didn't I tell ye? Ye'll be all right in a minit, and ez chipper ez a jay bird in the mornin'. Oh, don't tell me about rheumatics—I've bin thar! On'y mine was the cold kind—that hangs on longest—yours is the hot, that burns itself up in no time!"

If the flushed face and bright eyes of Lasham were not enough to corroborate this symptom of high fever, the quick, wandering laugh he gave would have indicated the point of delirium. But the too optimistic Daddy Folsom referred this act to improvement, and went on cheerfully: "Yes, sir, you're better now, and"—here he assumed an air of cautious deliberation, extravagant, as all his assumptions were—"I ain't sayin' that—ef—you—was—to—rise—up" (very slowly) "and heave a blanket or two over your shoulders— jest by way o' caution, you know—and leanin' on me, kinder meander over to Bob Falloner's cabin and the boys, it wouldn't do you a heap o' good. Changes o' this kind is often prescribed by the faculty." Another moan from the sufferer, however, here apparently corrected Daddy's too favorable prognosis. "Oh, all right! Well, perhaps ye know best; and I'll jest run over to Bob's and say how as ye ain't comin', and

Bret Harte

will be back in a jiffy!"

"The letter," said the sick man hurriedly, "the letter, the letter!"

Daddy leaned suddenly over the bed. It was impossible for even his hopefulness to avoid the fact that Lasham was delirious. It was a strong factor in the case—one that would certainly justify his going over to Falloner's with the news. For the present moment, however, this aberration was to be accepted cheerfully and humored after Daddy's own fashion. "Of course—the letter, the letter," he said convincingly; "that's what the boys hev bin singin' jest now—

'Good-by, Charley; when you are away,
Write me a letter, love; send me a letter, love!'

"That's what you heard, and a mighty purty song it is too, and kinder clings to you. It's wonderful how these things gets in your head."

"The letter—write—send money—money—money, and the photograph—the photograph—photograph—money," continued the sick man, in the rapid reiteration of delirium.

"In course you will—to-morrow—when the mail goes," returned Daddy soothingly; "plenty of them. Jest now you try to get a snooze, will ye? Hol' on!—take some o' this."

There was an anodyne mixture on the rude shelf, which the doctor had left on his morning visit. Daddy had a comfortable belief that what would relieve pain would also check delirium, and he accordingly measured out a dose with a liberal margin to allow of waste by the patient in swallowing in his semi-conscious state. As he lay more quiet, muttering still, but now unintelligibly, Daddy, waiting for a more complete unconsciousness and the opportunity to slip away to Falloner's, cast his eyes around the cabin. He noticed now for the first time since his entrance that a crumpled envelope bearing a Western post-mark was lying at the foot of the bed. Daddy knew that the tri-weekly post had arrived an hour before he came, and that Lasham had evidently received a letter. Sure enough the letter itself was lying against the wall beside him. It was open. Daddy felt justified in reading it.

It was curt and businesslike, stating that unless Lasham at once sent a remittance for the support of his brother and sister—two children in charge of the writer—they must find a home elsewhere. That the arrears were long standing, and the repeated promises of Lasham to send money had been unfulfilled. That the writer could stand it no longer. This would be his last communication unless the money were sent forthwith.

It was by no means a novel or, under the circumstances, a shocking disclosure to Daddy. He had seen similar missives from daughters, and even wives, consequent on the varying fortunes of his neighbors; no one knew better than he the uncertainties of a miner's prospects, and yet the inevitable hopefulness that buoyed him up. He tossed it aside impatiently, when his eye caught a strip of paper he had overlooked lying upon the blanket near the envelope. It contained a few lines in an unformed boyish hand addressed to "my brother," and evidently slipped into the letter after it was written. By the uncertain candlelight Daddy read as follows:—

Dear Brother, Rite to me and Cissy rite off. Why aint you done it? It's so long since you rote any. Mister Recketts ses you dont care any more. Wen you rite send your fotograff. Folks here ses I aint got no big bruther any way, as I disremember his looks, and cant say wots like him. Cissy's kryin' all along of it. I've got a hedake. William Walker make it ake by a blo. So no more at present from your loving little bruther Jim.

The quick, hysteric laugh with which Daddy read this was quite consistent with his responsive, emotional nature; so, too, were the ready tears that sprang to his eyes. He put the candle down unsteadily, with a casual glance at the sick man. It was notable, however, that this look contained less sympathy for the ailing "big brother" than his emotion might have suggested. For Daddy was carried quite away by his own mental picture of the helpless children, and eager only to relate his impressions of the incident. He cast another glance at the invalid, thrust the papers into his pocket, and clapping on his hat slipped from the cabin and ran to the house of festivity. Yet it was characteristic of the man, and so engrossed was he by his one idea, that to the usual inquiries regarding his patient he answered, "he's all right," and plunged at once into the incident of the dunning letter, reserving—with the instinct of an emotional artist—the child's missive until the last. As he expected, the money demand was received with indignant criticisms of the writer.

"That's just like 'em in the States," said Captain Fletcher; "darned if they don't believe we've only got to bore a hole in the ground and snake out a hundred dollars. Why, there's my wife—with a heap of hoss sense in everything else—is allus wonderin' why I can't rake in a cool fifty betwixt one steamer day and another."

"That's nothin' to my old dad," interrupted Gus Houston, the "infant" of the camp, a bright-eyed young fellow of twenty; "why, he wrote to me yesterday that if I'd only pick up a single piece of gold every day and just put it aside, sayin' 'That's for popper and mommer,' and not fool it away—it would be all they'd ask of me."

"That's so," added another; "these ignorant relations is just the ruin o' the mining industry. Bob Falloner hez bin lucky in his strike to-day, but he's a darned sight luckier in being without kith or kin that he knows of."

Daddy waited until the momentary irritation had subsided, and then drew the other letter from his pocket. "That ain't all, boys," he began in a faltering voice, but gradually working himself up to a pitch of pathos; "just as I was thinking all them very things, I kinder noticed this yer poor little bit o' paper lyin' thar lonesome like and forgotten, and I—read it—and well—gentlemen—it just choked me right up!" He stopped, and his voice faltered.

"Go slow, Daddy, go slow!" said an auditor smilingly. It was evident that Daddy's sympathetic weakness was well known.

Daddy read the child's letter. But, unfortunately, what with his real emotion and the intoxication of an audience, he read it extravagantly, and interpolated a child's lisp (on no authority whatever), and a simulated infantile delivery, which, I fear, at first provoked the smiles rather than the tears of his audience. Nevertheless, at its conclusion the little note was handed round the party, and then there was a moment of thoughtful silence.

"Tell you what it is, boys," said Fletcher, looking around the table, "we ought to be doin' suthin' for them kids right off! Did you," turning to Daddy, "say anythin' about this to Dick?"

"Nary—why, he's clean off his head with fever—don't understand a word—and just babbles," returned Daddy, forgetful of his roseate diagnosis a moment ago, "and hasn't got a cent."

"We must make up what we can amongst us afore the mail goes to-night," said the "infant," feeling hurriedly in his pockets. "Come, ante up, gentlemen," he added, laying the contents of his buckskin purse upon the table.

"Hold on, boys," said a quiet voice. It was their host Falloner, who had just risen and was slipping on his oilskin coat. "You've got enough to do, I reckon, to look after your own folks. I've none! Let this be my affair. I've got to go to the Express Office anyhow to see about my passage home, and I'll just get a draft for a hundred dollars for that old skeesicks—what's his blamed name? Oh, Ricketts"—he made a memorandum from the letter—"and I'll send it by express. Meantime, you fellows sit down there and write something—you know what—saying that Dick's hurt his hand and can't write—you know; but asked you to send a draft, which you're doing. Sabe? That's all! I'll skip over to the express now and get the draft off, and you can mail the letter an hour later. So put your dust back in your pockets and help yourselves to the whiskey while I'm gone." He clapped his hat on his head and disappeared.

"There goes a white man, you bet!" said Fletcher admiringly, as the door closed behind their host. "Now, boys," he added, drawing a chair to the table, "let's get this yer letter off, and then go back to our game."

Pens and ink were produced, and an animated discussion ensued as to the matter to be conveyed. Daddy's plea for an extended explanatory and sympathetic communication was overruled, and the letter was written to Ricketts on the simple lines suggested by Falloner.

"But what about poor little Jim's letter? That ought to be answered," said Daddy pathetically.

"If Dick hurt his hand so he can't write to Ricketts, how in thunder is he goin' to write to Jim?" was the reply.

"But suthin' oughter be said to the poor kid," urged Daddy piteously.

"Well, write it yourself—you and Gus Houston make up somethin' together. I'm going to win some money," retorted Fletcher, returning to the card-table, where he was presently followed by all but Daddy and Houston.

"Ye can't write it in Dick's name, because that little brother knows Dick's handwriting, even if he don't remember his face. See?" suggested Houston.

"That's so," said Daddy dubiously; "but," he added, with elastic cheerfulness, "we can write that Dick 'says.' See?"

"Your head's level, old man! Just you wade in on that."

Daddy seized the pen and "waded in." Into somewhat deep and difficult water, I fancy, for some of it splashed into his eyes, and he sniffled once or twice as he wrote. "Suthin' like this," he said, after a pause:—

DEAR LITTLE JIMMIE,—Your big brother havin' hurt his hand, wants me to tell you that otherways he is all hunky and A1. He says he don't forget you and little Cissy, you bet! and he's sendin' money to old Ricketts straight off. He says don't you and Cissy mind whether school keeps or not as long as big Brother Dick holds the lines. He says he'd have written before, but he's bin follerin' up a lead mighty close, and expects to strike it rich in a few days.

"You ain't got no sabe about kids," said Daddy imperturbably; "they've got to be humored like sick folks. And

Bret Harte

they want everythin' big—they don't take no stock in things ez they are—even ef they hev 'em worse than they are. 'So,'" continued Daddy, reading to prevent further interruption, "'he says you're just to keep your eyes skinned lookin' out for him comin' home any time—day or night. All you've got to do is to sit up and wait. He might come and even snake you out of your beds! He might come with four white horses and a nigger driver, or he might come disguised as an ornary tramp. Only you've got to be keen on watchin'.' (Ye see," interrupted Daddy explanatorily, "that'll jest keep them kids lively.) 'He says Cissy's to stop cryin' right off, and if Willie Walker hits yer on the right cheek you just slug out with your left fist, 'cordin' to Scripter.' Gosh," ejaculated Daddy, stopping suddenly and gazing anxiously at Houston, "there's that blamed photograph—I clean forgot that."

"And Dick hasn't got one in the shop, and never had," returned Houston emphatically. "Golly! that stumps us! Unless," he added, with diabolical thoughtfulness, "we take Bob's? The kids don't remember Dick's face, and Bob's about the same age. And it's a regular star picture—you bet! Bob had it taken in Sacramento—in all his war paint. See!" He indicated a photograph pinned against the wall—a really striking likeness which did full justice to Bob's long silken mustache and large, brown determined eyes. "I'll snake it off while they ain't lookin', and you jam it in the letter. Bob won't miss it, and we can fix it up with Dick after he's well, and send another."

Daddy silently grasped the "infant's" hand, who presently secured the photograph without attracting attention from the card-players. It was promptly inclosed in the letter, addressed to Master James Lasham. The "infant" started with it to the post-office, and Daddy Folsom returned to Lasham's cabin to relieve the watcher that had been detached from Falloner's to take his place beside the sick man.

Meanwhile the rain fell steadily and the shadows crept higher and higher up the mountain. Towards midnight the star points faded out one by one over Sawyer's Ledge even as they had come, with the difference that the illumination of Falloner's cabin was extinguished first, while the dim light of Lasham's increased in number. Later, two stars seemed to shoot from the centre of the ledge, trailing along the descent, until they were lost in the obscurity of the slope—the lights of the stage-coach to Sacramento carrying the mail and Robert Falloner. They met and passed two fainter lights toiling up the road—the buggy lights of the doctor, hastily summoned from Carterville to the bedside of the dying Dick Lasham.

The slowing up of his train caused Bob Falloner to start from a half doze in a Western Pullman car. As he glanced from his window he could see that the blinding snowstorm which had followed him for the past six hours had at last hopelessly blocked the line. There was no prospect beyond the interminable snowy level, the whirling flakes, and the monotonous palisades of leafless trees seen through it to the distant banks of the Missouri. It was a prospect that the mountain-bred Falloner was beginning to loathe, and although it was scarcely six weeks since he left California, he was already looking back regretfully to the deep slopes and the free song of the serried ranks of pines.

The intense cold had chilled his temperate blood, even as the rigors and conventions of Eastern life had checked his sincerity and spontaneous flow of animal spirits begotten in the frank intercourse and brotherhood of camps. He had just fled from the artificialities of the great Atlantic cities to seek out some Western farming lands in which he might put his capital and energies. The unlooked-for interruption of his progress by a long-forgotten climate only deepened his discontent. And now—that train was actually backing! It appeared they must return to the last station to wait for a snow-plough to clear the line. It was, explained the conductor, barely a mile from Shepherdstown, where there was a good hotel and a chance of breaking the journey for the night.

Shepherdstown! The name touched some dim chord in Bob Falloner's memory and conscience—yet one that was vague. Then he suddenly remembered that before leaving New York he had received a letter from Houston informing him of Lasham's death, reminding him of his previous bounty, and begging him—if he went West—to break the news to the Lasham family. There was also some allusion to a joke about his (Bob's) photograph, which he had dismissed as unimportant, and even now could not remember clearly. For a few moments his conscience pricked him that he should have forgotten it all, but now he could make amends by this providential delay. It was not a task to his liking; in any other circumstances he would have written, but he would not shirk it now.

Shepherdstown was on the main line of the Kansas Pacific Road, and as he alighted at its station, the big through trains from San Francisco swept out of the stormy distance and stopped also. He remembered, as he mingled with the passengers, hearing a childish voice ask if this was the Californian train. He remembered hearing the amused and patient reply of the station-master: "Yes, sonny—here she is again, and here's her passengers," as he got into the omnibus and drove to the hotel. Here he resolved to perform his disagreeable duty as quickly as possible, and on his way to his room stopped for a moment at the office to ask for Ricketts' address. The clerk, after a quick glance of curiosity at his new guest, gave it to him readily, with a somewhat familiar smile. It struck Falloner also as being odd that he had not been asked to write his name on the hotel register, but this was a saving of time he was not disposed to question, as he had already determined to make his visit to Ricketts at once, before dinner. It was still early evening.

He was washing his hands in his bedroom when there came a light tap at his sitting-room door. Falloner quickly resumed his coat and entered the sitting-room as the porter ushered in a young lady holding a small boy by the hand. But, to Falloner's utter consternation, no sooner had the door closed on the servant than the boy, with a half-apologetic glance at the young lady, uttered a childish cry, broke from her, and calling, "Dick! Dick!" ran forward and leaped into Falloner's arms.

The mere shock of the onset and his own amazement left Bob without breath for words. The boy, with arms convulsively clasping his body, was imprinting kisses on Bob's waistcoat in default of reaching his face. At last Falloner managed gently but firmly to free himself, and turned a half-appealing, half-embarrassed look upon the young lady, whose own face, however, suddenly flushed pink. To add to the confusion, the boy, in some reaction of instinct, suddenly ran back to her, frantically clutched at her skirts, and tried to bury his head in their folds.

"He don't love me," he sobbed. "He don't care for me any more."

The face of the young girl changed. It was a pretty face in its flushing; in the paleness and thoughtfulness that overcast it it was a striking face, and Bob's attention was for a moment distracted from the grotesqueness of the situation. Leaning over the boy she said in a caressing yet authoritative voice, "Run away for a moment, dear, until I call you," opening the door for him in a maternal way so inconsistent with the youthfulness of her figure that it struck him even in his confusion. There was something also in her dress and carriage that equally affected him: her garments were somewhat old-fashioned in style, yet of good material, with an odd incongruity to the climate and season.

Under her rough outer cloak she wore a polka jacket and the thinnest of summer blouses; and her hat, though dark, was of rough straw, plainly trimmed. Nevertheless, these peculiarities were carried off with an air of breeding and self-possession that was unmistakable. It was possible that her cool self-possession might have been due to some instinctive antagonism, for as she came a step forward with coldly and clearly-opened gray eyes, he was vaguely conscious that she didn't like him. Nevertheless, her manner was formally polite, even, as he fancied, to the point of irony, as she began, in a voice that occasionally dropped into the lazy Southern intonation, and a speech that easily slipped at times into Southern dialect:—

"I sent the child out of the room, as I could see that his advances were annoying to you, and a good deal, I reckon, because I knew your reception of them was still more painful to him. It is quite natural, I dare say, you should feel as you do, and I reckon consistent with your attitude towards him. But you must make some allowance for the depth of his feelings, and how he has looked forward to this meeting. When I tell you that ever since he received your last letter, he and his sister—until her illness kept her home—have gone every day when the Pacific train was due to the station to meet you; that they have taken literally as Gospel truth every word of your letter"—

"My letter?" interrupted Falloner.

The young girl's scarlet lip curled slightly. "I beg your pardon—I should have said the letter you dictated. Of course it wasn't in your handwriting—you had hurt your hand, you know," she added ironically. "At all events, they believed it all—that you were coming at any moment; they lived in that belief, and the poor things went to the station with your photograph in their hands so that they might be the first to recognize and greet you."

"With my photograph?" interrupted Falloner again.

The young girl's clear eyes darkened ominously. "I reckon," she said deliberately, as she slowly drew from her pocket the photograph Daddy Folsom had sent, "that that is your photograph. It certainly seems an excellent likeness," she added, regarding him with a slight suggestion of contemptuous triumph.

In an instant the revelation of the whole mystery flashed upon him! The forgotten passage in Houston's letter about the stolen photograph stood clearly before him; the coincidence of his appearance in Shepherdstown, and the natural mistake of the children and their fair protector, were made perfectly plain. But with this relief and the certainty that he could confound her with an explanation came a certain mischievous desire to prolong the situation and increase his triumph. She certainly had not shown him any favor.

"Have you got the letter also?" he asked quietly.

She whisked it impatiently from her pocket and handed it to him. As he read Daddy's characteristic extravagance and recognized the familiar idiosyncrasies of his old companions, he was unable to restrain a smile. He raised his eyes, to meet with surprise the fair stranger's leveled eyebrows and brightly indignant eyes, in which, however, the rain was fast gathering with the lightning.

Bret Harte

"It may be amusing to you, and I reckon likely it was all a California joke," she said with slightly trembling lips; "I don't know No'thern gentlemen and their ways, and you seem to have forgotten our ways as you have your kindred. Perhaps all this may seem so funny to them: it may not seem funny to that boy who is now crying his heart out in the hall; it may not be very amusing to that poor Cissy in her sick-bed longing to see her brother. It may be so far from amusing to her, that I should hesitate to bring you there in her excited condition and subject her to the pain that you have caused him. But I have promised her; she is already expecting us, and the disappointment may be dangerous, and I can only implore you—for a few moments at least—to show a little more affection than you feel." As he made an impulsive, deprecating gesture, yet without changing his look of restrained amusement, she stopped him hopelessly. "Oh, of course, yes, yes, I know it is years since you have seen them; they have no right to expect more; only—only—feeling as you do," she burst impulsively, "why—oh, why did you come?"

Here was Bob's chance. He turned to her politely; began gravely, "I simply came to"—when suddenly his face changed; he stopped as if struck by a blow. His cheek flushed, and then paled! Good God! What had he come for? To tell them that this brother they were longing for—living for—perhaps even dying for—was dead! In his crass stupidity, his wounded vanity over the scorn of the young girl, his anticipation of triumph, he had forgotten—totally forgotten—what that triumph meant! Perhaps if he had felt more keenly the death of Lasham the thought of it would have been uppermost in his mind; but Lasham was not his partner or associate, only a brother miner, and his single act of generosity was in the ordinary routine of camp life. If she could think him cold and heartless before, what would she think of him now? The absurdity of her mistake had vanished in the grim tragedy he had seemed to have cruelly prepared for her. The thought struck him so keenly that he stammered, faltered, and sank helplessly into a chair.

The shock that he had received was so plain to her that her own indignation went out in the breath of it. Her lip quivered. "Don't you mind," she said hurriedly, dropping into her Southern speech; "I didn't go to hurt you, but I was just that mad with the thought of those pickaninnies, and the easy way you took it, that I clean forgot I'd no call to catechise you! And you don't know me from the Queen of Sheba. Well," she went on, still more rapidly, and in odd distinction to her previous formal slow Southern delivery, "I'm the daughter of Colonel Boutelle, of Bayou Sara, Louisiana; and his paw, and his paw before him, had a plantation there since the time of Adam, but he lost it and six hundred niggers during the Wah! We were pooh as pohverty—paw and maw and we four girls—and no more idea of work than a baby. But I had an education at the convent at New Orleans, and could play, and speak French, and I got a place as school-teacher here; I reckon the first Southern woman that has taught school in the No'th! Ricketts, who used to be our steward at Bayou Sara, told me about the pickaninnies, and how helpless they were, with only a brother who occasionally sent them money from California. I suppose I cottoned to the pooh little things at first because I knew what it was to be alone amongst strangers, Mr. Lasham; I used to teach them at odd times, and look after them, and go with them to the train to look for you. Perhaps Ricketts made me think you didn't care for them; perhaps I was wrong in thinking it was true, from the way you met Jimmy just now. But I've spoken my mind and you know why." She ceased and walked to the window.

Falloner rose. The storm that had swept through him was over. The quick determination, resolute purpose, and infinite patience which had made him what he was were all there, and with it a conscientiousness which his selfish independence had hitherto kept dormant. He accepted the situation, not passively—it was not in his nature—but threw himself into it with all his energy.

"You were quite right," he said, halting a moment beside her; "I don't blame you, and let me hope that later you may think me less to blame than you do now. Now, what's to be done? Clearly, I've first to make it right with Tommy—I mean Jimmy—and then we must make a straight dash over to the girl! Whoop!" Before she could understand from his face the strange change in his voice, he had dashed out of the room. In a moment he reappeared with the boy struggling in his arms. "Think of the little scamp not knowing his own brother!" he laughed, giving the boy a really affectionate, if slightly exaggerated hug, "and expecting me to open my arms to the first little boy who jumps into them! I've a great mind not to give him the present I fetched all the way from California. Wait a moment." He dashed into the bedroom, opened his valise—where he providentially remembered he had kept, with a miner's superstition, the first little nugget of gold he had ever found—seized the tiny bit of quartz of gold, and dashed out again to display it before Jimmy's eager eyes.

If the heartiness, sympathy, and charming kindness of the man's whole manner and face convinced, even while it slightly startled, the young girl, it was still more effective with the boy. Children are quick to detect the false ring of affected emotion, and Bob's was so genuine—whatever its cause—that it might have easily passed for a fraternal expression with harder critics. The child trustfully nestled against him and would have grasped the gold, but the young man whisked it into his pocket. "Not until we've shown it to our little sister—where we're going now! I'm off to order a sleigh." He dashed out again to the office as if he found some relief in action, or, as it seemed to Miss Boutelle, to avoid embarrassing conversation. When he came back again he was carrying an immense bearskin from his luggage. He cast a critical look at the girl's unseasonable attire.

"I shall wrap you and Jimmy in this—you know it's snowing frightfully."

Miss Boutelle flushed a little. "I'm warm enough when walking," she said coldly. Bob glanced at her smart little French shoes, and thought otherwise. He said nothing, but hastily bundled his two guests downstairs and into the street. The whirlwind dance of the snow made the sleigh an indistinct bulk in the glittering darkness, and as the young girl for an instant stood dazedly still, Bob incontinently lifted her from her feet, deposited her in the vehicle, dropped Jimmy in her lap, and wrapped them both tightly in the bearskin. Her weight, which was scarcely more than a child's, struck him in that moment as being tantalizingly incongruous to the matronly severity of her manner and its strange effect upon him. He then jumped in himself, taking the direction from his companion, and drove off through the storm.

The wind and darkness were not favorable to conversation, and only once did he break the silence. "Is there any one who would be likely to remember—me—where we are going?" he asked, in a lull of the storm.

Miss Boutelle uncovered enough of her face to glance at him curiously. "Hardly! You know the children came here from the No'th after your mother's death, while you were in California."

"Of course," returned Bob hurriedly; "I was only thinking— you know that some of my old friends might have called," and then collapsed into silence.

After a pause a voice came icily, although under the furs: "Perhaps you'd prefer that your arrival be kept secret from the public? But they seem to have already recognized you at the hotel from your inquiry about Ricketts, and the photograph Jimmy had already shown them two weeks ago." Bob remembered the clerk's familiar manner and the omission to ask him to register. "But it need go no further, if you like," she added, with a slight return of her previous scorn.

"I've no reason for keeping it secret," said Bob stoutly.

No other words were exchanged until the sleigh drew up before a plain wooden house in the suburbs of the town. Bob could see at a glance that it represented the income of some careful artisan or small shopkeeper, and that it promised little for an invalid's luxurious comfort. They were ushered into a chilly sitting-room and Miss Boutelle ran upstairs with Jimmy to prepare the invalid for Bob's appearance. He noticed that a word dropped by the woman who opened the door made the young girl's face grave again, and paled the color that the storm had buffeted to her cheek. He noticed also that these plain surroundings seemed only to enhance her own superiority, and that the woman treated her with a deference in odd contrast to the ill-concealed disfavor with which she regarded him. Strangely enough, this latter fact was a relief to his conscience. It would have been terrible to have received their kindness under false pretenses; to take their just blame of the man he personated seemed to mitigate the deceit.

The young girl rejoined him presently with troubled eyes. Cissy was worse, and only intermittently conscious, but had asked to see him. It was a short flight of stairs to the bedroom, but before he reached it Bob's heart beat faster than it had in any mountain climb. In one corner of the plainly furnished room stood a small truckle bed, and in it lay the invalid. It needed but a single glance at her flushed face in its aureole of yellow hair to recognize the likeness to Jimmy, although, added to that strange refinement produced by suffering, there was a spiritual exaltation in the child's look—possibly from delirium—that awed and frightened him; an awful feeling that he could not lie to this hopeless creature took possession of him, and his step faltered. But she lifted her small arms pathetically towards him as if she divined his trouble, and he sank on his knees beside her. With a tiny finger curled around his long mustache, she lay there silent. Her face was full of trustfulness, happiness, and consciousness—but she spoke no word.

There was a pause, and Falloner, slightly lifting his head without disturbing that faintly clasping finger, beckoned Miss Boutelle to his side. "Can you drive?" he said, in a low voice.

"Yes."

"Take my sleigh and get the best doctor in town to come here at once. Bring him with you if you can; if he can't come at once, drive home yourself. I will stay here."

"But"—hesitated Miss Boutelle.

"I will stay here," he repeated.

The door closed on the young girl, and Falloner, still bending over the child, presently heard the sleigh-bells pass away in the storm. He still sat with his bent head, held by the tiny clasp of those thin fingers. But the child's eyes were fixed so intently upon him that Mrs. Ricketts leaned over the strangely-assorted pair and said—

"It's your brother Dick, dearie. Don't you know him?"

Bret Harte

The child's lips moved faintly. "Dick's dead," she whispered.

"She's wandering," said Mrs. Ricketts. "Speak to her." But Bob, with his eyes on the child's, lifted a protesting hand. The little sufferer's lips moved again. "It isn't Dick—it's the angel God sent to tell me."

She spoke no more. And when Miss Boutelle returned with the doctor she was beyond the reach of finite voices. Falloner would have remained all night with them, but he could see that his presence in the contracted household was not desired. Even his offer to take Jimmy with him to the hotel was declined, and at midnight he returned alone.

What his thoughts were that night may be easily imagined. Cissy's death had removed the only cause he had for concealing his real identity. There was nothing more to prevent his revealing all to Miss Boutelle and to offer to adopt the boy. But he reflected this could not be done until after the funeral, for it was only due to Cissy's memory that he should still keep up the role of Dick Lasham as chief mourner. If it seems strange that Bob did not at this crucial moment take Miss Boutelle into his confidence, I fear it was because he dreaded the personal effect of the deceit he had practiced upon her more than any ethical consideration; she had softened considerably in her attitude towards him that night; he was human, after all, and while he felt his conduct had been unselfish in the main, he dared not confess to himself how much her opinion had influenced him. He resolved that after the funeral he would continue his journey, and write to her, en route, a full explanation of his conduct, inclosing Daddy's letter as corroborative evidence. But on searching his letter-case he found that he had lost even that evidence, and he must trust solely at present to her faith in his improbable story.

It seemed as if his greatest sacrifice was demanded at the funeral! For it could not be disguised that the neighbors were strongly prejudiced against him. Even the preacher improved the occasion to warn the congregation against the dangers of putting off duty until too late. And when Robert Falloner, pale, but self-restrained, left the church with Miss Boutelle, equally pale and reserved, on his arm, he could with difficulty restrain his fury at the passing of a significant smile across the faces of a few curious bystanders. "It was Amy Boutelle, that was the 'penitence' that fetched him, you bet!" he overheard, a barely concealed whisper; and the reply, "And it's a good thing she's made out of it too, for he's mighty rich!"

At the church door he took her cold hand into his. "I am leaving to-morrow morning with Jimmy," he said, with a white face. "Good-by."

"You are quite right; good-by," she replied as briefly, but with the faintest color. He wondered if she had heard it too.

Whether she had heard it or not, she went home with Mrs. Ricketts in some righteous indignation, which found—after the young lady's habit—free expression. Whatever were Mr. Lasham's faults of omission it was most un-Christian to allude to them there, and an insult to the poor little dear's memory who had forgiven them. Were she in his shoes she would shake the dust of the town off her feet; and she hoped he would. She was a little softened on arriving to find Jimmy in tears. He had lost Dick's photograph—or Dick had forgotten to give it back at the hotel, for this was all he had in his pocket. And he produced a letter—the missing letter of Daddy, which by mistake Falloner had handed back instead of the photograph. Miss Boutelle saw the superscription and Californian postmark with a vague curiosity.

"Did you look inside, dear? Perhaps it slipped in."

Jimmy had not. Miss Boutelle did—and I grieve to say, ended by reading the whole letter.

Bob Falloner had finished packing his things the next morning, and was waiting for Mr. Ricketts and Jimmy. But when a tap came at the door, he opened it to find Miss Boutelle standing there. "I have sent Jimmy into the bedroom," she said with a faint smile, "to look for the photograph which you gave him in mistake for this. I think for the present he prefers his brother's picture to this letter, which I have not explained to him or any one." She stopped, and raising her eyes to his, said gently: "I think it would have only been a part of your goodness to have trusted me, Mr. Falloner."

"Then you will forgive me?" he said eagerly.

She looked at him frankly, yet with a faint trace of coquetry that the angels might have pardoned. "Do you want me to say to you what Mrs. Ricketts says were the last words of poor Cissy?"

A year later, when the darkness and rain were creeping up Sawyer's Ledge, and Houston and Daddy Folsom were sitting before their brushwood fire in the old Lasham cabin, the latter delivered himself oracularly.

"It's a mighty queer thing, that news about Bob! It's not that he's married, for that might happen to any one; but this yer account in the paper of his wedding being attended by his 'little brother.' That gets me! To think all the while he was here he was lettin' on to us that he hadn't kith or kin! Well, sir, that accounts to me for one thing,—the sing'ler way he tumbled to that letter of poor Dick Lasham's little brother and sent him that draft! Don't ye see? It was a feller feelin'! Knew how it was himself! I reckon ye all thought I was kinder soft reading that letter o' Dick Lasham's little brother to him, but ye see what it did."

Bret Harte

THE YOUNGEST MISS PIPER

I do not think that any of us who enjoyed the acquaintance of the Piper girls or the hospitality of Judge Piper, their father, ever cared for the youngest sister. Not on account of her extreme youth, for the eldest Miss Piper confessed to twenty-six—and the youth of the youngest sister was established solely, I think, by one big braid down her back. Neither was it because she was the plainest, for the beauty of the Piper girls was a recognized general distinction, and the youngest Miss Piper was not entirely devoid of the family charms. Nor was it from any lack of intelligence, nor from any defective social quality; for her precocity was astounding, and her good-humored frankness alarming. Neither do I think it could be said that a slight deafness, which might impart an embarrassing publicity to any statement—the reverse of our general feeling—that might be confided by any one to her private ear, was a sufficient reason; for it was pointed out that she always understood everything that Tom Sparrell told her in his ordinary tone of voice. Briefly, it was very possible that Delaware—the youngest Miss Piper—did not like us. Yet it was fondly believed by us that the other sisters failed to show that indifference to our existence shown by Miss Delaware, although the heartburnings, misunderstandings, jealousies, hopes and fears, and finally the chivalrous resignation with which we at last accepted the long foregone conclusion that they were not for us, and far beyond our reach, is not a part of this veracious chronicle. Enough that none of the flirtations of her elder sisters affected or were shared by the youngest Miss Piper. She moved in this heart-breaking atmosphere with sublime indifference, treating her sisters' affairs with what we considered rank simplicity or appalling frankness. Their few admirers who were weak enough to attempt to gain her mediation or confidence had reason to regret it.

"It's no kind o' use givin' me goodies," she said to a helpless suitor of Louisiana Piper's who had offered to bring her some sweets, "for I ain't got no influence with Lu, and if I don't give 'em up to her when she hears of it, she'll nag me and hate you like pizen. Unless," she added thoughtfully, "it was wintergreen lozenges; Lu can't stand them, or anybody who eats them within a mile." It is needless to add that the miserable man, thus put upon his gallantry, was obliged in honor to provide Del with the wintergreen lozenges that kept him in disfavor and at a distance. Unfortunately, too, any predilection or pity for any particular suitor of her sister's was attended by even more disastrous consequences. It was reported that while acting as "gooseberry"—a role usually assigned to her—between Virginia Piper and an exceptio-nally timid young surveyor, during a ramble she conceived a rare sentiment of humanity towards the unhappy man. After once or twice lingering behind in the ostentatious picking of a wayside flower, or "running on ahead" to look at a mountain view, without any apparent effect on the shy and speechless youth, she decoyed him aside while her elder sister rambled indifferently and somewhat scornfully on. The youngest Miss Piper leaped upon the rail of a fence, and with the stalk of a thimbleberry in her mouth swung her small feet to and fro and surveyed him dispassionately.

"Ye don't seem to be ketchin' on?" she said tentatively.

The young man smiled feebly and interrogatively.

"Don't seem to be either follering suit nor trumpin'," continued Del bluntly.

"I suppose so—that is, I fear that Miss Virginia"—he stammered.

"Speak up! I'm a little deaf. Say it again!" said Del, screwing up her eyes and eyebrows.

The young man was obliged to admit in stentorian tones that his progress had been scarcely satisfactory.

"You're goin' on too slow—that's it," said Del critically. "Why, when Captain Savage meandered along here with Jinny" (Virginia) "last week, afore we got as far as this he'd reeled off a heap of Byron and Jamieson" (Tennyson), "and sich; and only yesterday Jinny and Doctor Beveridge was blowin' thistletops to know which was a flirt all along the trail past the crossroads. Why, ye ain't picked ez much as a single berry for Jinny, let alone Lad's Love or Johnny Jumpups and Kissme's, and ye keep talkin' across me, you two, till I'm tired. Now look here," she burst out with sudden decision, "Jinny's gone on ahead in a kind o' huff; but I reckon she's done that afore too, and you'll find her, jest as Spinner did, on the rise of the hill, sittin' on a pine stump and lookin' like this." (Here the youngest Miss Piper locked her fingers over her left knee, and drew it slightly up,—with a sublime indifference to the exposure of considerable small-ankled red stocking,—and with a far-off, plaintive stare, achieved a colorable imitation of her elder sister's probable attitude.) "Then you jest go up softly, like as you was a bear, and clap your hands on her eyes, and say in a disguised voice like this" (here Del turned on a high falsetto beyond any masculine compass), "'Who's who?' jest like in forfeits."

"But she'll be sure to know me," said the surveyor timidly.

"She won't," said Del in scornful skepticism.

"I hardly think"—stammered the young man, with an awkward smile, "that I—in fact—she'll discover me—before I can get beside her."

"Not if you go softly, for she'll be sittin' back to the road, so —gazing away, so"—the youngest Miss Piper again stared dreamily in the distance, "and you'll creep up just behind, like this."

"But won't she be angry? I haven't known her long—that is —don't you see?" He stopped embarrassedly.

"Can't hear a word you say," said Del, shaking her head decisively. "You've got my deaf ear. Speak louder, or come closer."

But here the instruction suddenly ended, once and for all time! For whether the young man was seriously anxious to perfect himself; whether he was truly grateful to the young girl and tried to show it; whether he was emboldened by the childish appeal of the long brown distinguishing braid down her back, or whether he suddenly found something peculiarly provocative in the reddish brown eyes between their thickset hedge of lashes, and with the trim figure and piquant pose, and was seized with that hysteric desperation which sometimes attacks timidity itself, I cannot say! Enough that he suddenly put his arm around her waist and his lips to her soft satin cheek, peppered and salted as it was by sun-freckles and mountain air, and received a sound box on the ear for his pains. The incident was closed. He did not repeat the experiment on either sister. The disclosure of his rebuff seemed, however, to give a singular satisfaction to Red Gulch.

While it may be gathered from this that the youngest Miss Piper was impervious to general masculine advances, it was not until later that Red Gulch was thrown into skeptical astonishment by the rumors that all this time she really had a lover! Allusion has been made to the charge that her deafness did not prevent her from perfectly understanding the ordinary tone of voice of a certain Mr. Thomas Sparrell.

No undue significance was attached to this fact through the very insignificance and "impossibility" of that individual;—a lanky, red-haired youth, incapacitated for manual labor through lameness,—a clerk in a general store at the Cross Roads! He had never been the recipient of Judge Piper's hospitality; he had never visited the house even with parcels; apparently his only interviews with her or any of the family had been over the counter. To do him justice he certainly had never seemed to seek any nearer acquaintance; he was not at the church door when her sisters, beautiful in their Sunday gowns, filed into the aisle, with little Delaware bringing up the rear; he was not at the Democratic barbecue, that we attended without reference to our personal politics, and solely for the sake of Judge Piper and the girls; nor did he go to the Agricultural Fair Ball—open to all. His abstention we believed to be owing to his lameness; to a wholesome consciousness of his own social defects; or an inordinate passion for reading cheap scientific textbooks, which did not, however, add fluency nor conviction to his speech. Neither had he the abstraction of a student, for his accounts were kept with an accuracy which struck us, who dealt at the store, as ignobly practical, and even malignant. Possibly we might have expressed this opinion more strongly but for a certain rude vigor of repartee which he possessed, and a suggestion that he might have a temper on occasion. "Them red-haired chaps is like to be tetchy and to kinder see blood through their eyelashes," had been suggested by an observing customer.

In short, little as we knew of the youngest Miss Piper, he was the last man we should have suspected her to select as an admirer. What we did know of their public relations, purely commercial ones, implied the reverse of any cordial understanding. The provisioning of the Piper household was entrusted to Del, with other practical odds and ends of housekeeping, not ornamental, and the following is said to be a truthful record of one of their overheard interviews at the store:—

The youngest Miss Piper, entering, displacing a quantity of goods in the centre to make a sideways seat for herself, and looking around loftily as she took a memorandum-book and pencil from her pocket.

"Ahem! If I ain't taking you away from your studies, Mr. Sparrell, maybe you'll be good enough to look here a minit;—but" (in affected politeness) "if I'm disturbing you I can come another time."

Sparrell, placing the book he had been reading carefully under the counter, and advancing to Miss Delaware with a complete ignoring of her irony: "What can we do for you to-day, Miss Piper?"

Miss Delaware, with great suavity of manner, examining her memorandum-book: "I suppose it wouldn't be shocking your delicate feelings too much to inform you that the canned lobster and oysters you sent us yesterday wasn't fit for hogs?"

Sparrell (blandly): "They weren't intended for them, Miss Piper. If we had known you were having company over from Red Gulch to dinner, we might have provided something more suitable for them. We have a fair quality of oil-cake and corn-cobs in stock, at reduced figures. But the canned provisions were for your own family."

Miss Delaware (secretly pleased at this sarcastic allusion to her sister's friends, but concealing her delight): "I admire to hear you talk that way, Mr. Sparrell; it's better than minstrels or a circus. I suppose you get it outer that book," indicating the concealed volume. "What do you call it?"

Sparrell (politely): "The First Principles of Geology."

Miss Delaware, leaning sideways and curling her little fingers around her pink ear: "Did you say the first principles of 'geology' or 'politeness'? You know I am so deaf; but, of course, it couldn't be that."

Sparrell (easily): "Oh no, you seem to have that in your hand"—pointing to Miss Delaware's memorandum-book—"you were quoting from it when you came in."

Miss Delaware, after an affected silence of deep resignation: "Well! it's too bad folks can't just spend their lives listenin' to such elegant talk; I'd admire to do nothing else! But there's my family up at Cottonwood—and they must eat. They're that low that they expect me to waste my time getting food for 'em here, instead of drinking in the First Principles of the Grocery."

"Geology," suggested Sparrell blandly. "The history of rock formation."

"Geology," accepted Miss Delaware apologetically; "the history of rocks, which is so necessary for knowing just how much sand you can put in the sugar. So I reckon I'll leave my list here, and you can have the things toted to Cottonwood when you've got through with your First Principles."

She tore out a list of her commissions from a page of her memorandum-book, leaped lightly from the counter, threw her brown braid from her left shoulder to its proper place down her back, shook out her skirts deliberately, and saying, "Thank you for a most improvin' afternoon, Mr. Sparrell," sailed demurely out of the store.

A few auditors of this narrative thought it inconsistent that a daughter of Judge Piper and a sister of the angelic host should put up with a mere clerk's familiarity, but it was pointed out that "she gave him as good as he sent," and the story was generally credited. But certainly no one ever dreamed that it pointed to any more precious confidences between them.

I think the secret burst upon the family, with other things, at the big picnic at Reservoir Canyon. This festivity had been arranged for weeks previously, and was undertaken chiefly by the "Red Gulch Contingent," as we were called, as a slight return to the Piper family for their frequent hospitality. The Piper sisters were expected to bring nothing but their own personal graces and attend to the ministration of such viands and delicacies as the boys had profusely supplied.

The site selected was Reservoir Canyon, a beautiful, triangular valley with very steep sides, one of which was crowned by the immense reservoir of the Pioneer Ditch Company. The sheer flanks of the canyon descended in furrowed lines of vines and clinging bushes, like folds of falling skirts, until they broke again into flounces of spangled shrubbery over a broad level carpet of monkshood, mariposas, lupines, poppies, and daisies. Tempered and secluded from the sun's rays by its lofty shadows, the delicious obscurity of the canyon was in sharp contrast to the fiery mountain trail that in the full glare of the noonday sky made its tortuous way down the hillside, like a stream of lava, to plunge suddenly into the valley and extinguish itself in its coolness as in a lake. The heavy odors of wild honeysuckle, syringa, and ceanothus that hung over it were lightened and freshened by the sharp spicing of pine and bay. The mountain breeze which sometimes shook the serrated tops of the large redwoods above with a chill from the remote snow peaks even in the heart of summer, never reached the little valley.

It seemed an ideal place for a picnic. Everybody was therefore astonished to hear that an objection was suddenly raised to this perfect site. They were still more astonished to know that the objector was the youngest Miss Piper! Pressed to give her reasons, she had replied that the locality was dangerous; that the reservoir placed upon the mountain, notoriously old and worn out, had been rendered more unsafe by false economy in unskillful and hasty repairs to satisfy speculating stockbrokers, and that it had lately shown signs of leakage and sapping of its outer walls; that, in the event of an outbreak, the little triangular valley, from which there was no outlet, would be instantly flooded. Asked still more pressingly to give her authority for these details, she at first hesitated, and then gave the name of Tom Sparrell.

The derision with which this statement was received by us all, as the opinion of a sedentary clerk, was quite natural and obvious, but not the anger which it excited in the breast of Judge Piper; for it was not generally known that the judge was the holder of a considerable number of shares in the Pioneer Ditch Company, and that large dividends had been lately kept up by a false economy of expenditure, to expedite a "sharp deal" in the stock, by which the judge and others could sell out of a failing company. Rather, it was believed, that the judge's anger was due only to the discovery of Sparrell's influence over his daughter and his interference with the social affairs of Cottonwood. It was said that there was a sharp scene between the youngest Miss Piper and the combined forces of the judge and the elder sisters, which ended in the former's resolute refusal to attend the picnic at all if that site was selected.

As Delaware was known to be fearless even to the point of recklessness, and fond of gayety, her refusal only intensified the belief that she was merely "stickin' up for Sparrell's judgment" without any reference to her own personal safety or that of her sisters. The warning was laughed away; the opinion of Sparrell treated with ridicule as the dyspeptic and envious expression of an impractical man. It was pointed out that the reservoir had lasted a long time even in its alleged ruinous state; that only a miracle of coincidence could make it break down that particular afternoon of the picnic; that even if it did happen, there was no direct proof that it would seriously flood the valley, or at best add more than a spice of excitement to the affair. The "Red Gulch Contingent," who WOULD be there, was quite as capable of taking care of the ladies, in case of any accident, as any lame crank who wouldn't, but could only croak a warning to them from a distance. A few even wished something might happen that they might have an opportunity of showing their superior devotion; indeed, the prospect of carrying the half-submerged sisters, in a condition of helpless loveliness, in their arms to a place of safety was a fascinating possibility. The warning was conspicuously ineffective; everybody looked eagerly forward to the day and the unchanged locality; to the greatest hopefulness and anticipation was added the stirring of defiance, and when at last the appointed hour had arrived, the picnic party passed down the twisting mountain trail through the heat and glare in a fever of enthusiasm.

It was a pretty sight to view this sparkling procession—the girls cool and radiant in their white, blue, and yellow muslins and flying ribbons, the "Contingent" in its cleanest ducks, and blue and red flannel shirts, the judge white-waistcoated and panama-hatted, with a new dignity borrowed from the previous circumstances, and three or four impressive Chinamen bringing up the rear with hampers—as it at last debouched into Reservoir Canyon.

Here they dispersed themselves over the limited area, scarcely half an acre, with the freedom of escaped school children. They were secure in their woodland privacy. They were overlooked by no high road and its passing teams; they were safe from accidental intrusion from the settlement; indeed they went so far as to effect the exclusiveness of "clique." At first they amused themselves by casting humorously defiant eyes at the long low Ditch Reservoir, which peeped over the green wall of the ridge, six hundred feet above them; at times they even simulated an exaggerated terror of it, and one recognized humorist declaimed a grotesque appeal to its forbearance, with delightful local allusions. Others pretended to discover near a woodman's hut, among the belt of pines at the top of the descending trail, the peeping figure of the ridiculous and envious Sparrell. But all this was presently forgotten in the actual festivity. Small as was the range of the valley, it still allowed retreats during the dances for waiting couples among the convenient laurel and manzanita bushes which flounced the mountain side. After the dancing, old-fashioned children's games were revived with great laughter and half-hearted and coy protests from the ladies; notably one pastime known as "I'm a-pinin'," in which ingenious performance the victim was obliged to stand in the centre of a circle and publicly "pine" for a member of the opposite sex. Some hilarity was occasioned by the mischievous Miss "Georgy" Piper declaring, when it came to her turn, that she was "pinin'" for a look at the face of Tom Sparrell just now!

In this local trifling two hours passed, until the party sat down to the long-looked for repast. It was here that the health of Judge Piper was neatly proposed by the editor of the "Argus." The judge responded with great dignity and some emotion. He reminded them that it had been his humble endeavor to promote harmony—that harmony so characteristic of American principles—in social as he had in political circles, and particularly among the strangely constituted yet purely American elements of frontier life. He accepted the present festivity with its overflowing hospitalities, not in recognition of himself—("yes! yes!")—nor of his family—(enthusiastic protests)—but of that American principle! If at one time it seemed probable that these festivities might be marred by the machinations of envy—(groans)—or that harmony interrupted by the importation of low-toned material interests—(groans)—he could say that, looking around him, he had never before felt—er—that— Here the judge stopped short, reeled slightly forward, caught at a camp-stool, recovered himself with an apologetic smile, and turned inquiringly to his neighbor.

A light laugh—instantly suppressed—at what was at first supposed to be the effect of the "overflowing hospitality" upon the speaker himself, went around the male circle until it suddenly appeared that half a dozen others had started to their feet at the same time, with white faces, and that one of the ladies had screamed.

"What is it?" everybody was asking with interrogatory smiles.

It was Judge Piper who replied:—

"A little shock of earthquake," he said blandly; "a mere thrill! I think," he added with a faint smile, "we may say that Nature herself has applauded our efforts in good old Californian fashion, and signified her assent. What are you

Bret Harte

saying, Fludder?"

"I was thinking, sir," said Fludder deferentially, in a lower voice, "that if anything was wrong in the reservoir, this shock, you know, might"—

He was interrupted by a faint crashing and crackling sound, and looking up, beheld a good-sized boulder, evidently detached from some greater height, strike the upland plateau at the left of the trail and bound into the fringe of forest beside it. A slight cloud of dust marked its course, and then lazily floated away in mid air. But it had been watched agitatedly, and it was evident that that singular loss of nervous balance which is apt to affect all those who go through the slightest earthquake experience was felt by all. But some sense of humor, however, remained.

"Looks as if the water risks we took ain't goin' to cover earthquakes," drawled Dick Frisney; "still that wasn't a bad shot, if we only knew what they were aiming at."

"Do be quiet," said Virginia Piper, her cheeks pink with excitement. "Listen, can't you? What's that funny murmuring you hear now and then up there?"

"It's only the snow-wind playin' with the pines on the summit. You girls won't allow anybody any fun but yourselves."

But here a scream from "Georgy," who, assisted by Captain Fairfax, had mounted a camp-stool at the mouth of the valley, attracted everybody's attention. She was standing upright, with dilated eyes, staring at the top of the trail. "Look!" she said excitedly, "if the trail isn't moving!"

Everybody faced in that direction. At the first glance it

seemed indeed as if the trail was actually moving; wriggling and undulating its tortuous way down the mountain like a huge snake, only swollen to twice its usual size. But the second glance showed it to be no longer a trail but a channel of water, whose stream, lifted in a bore-like wall four or five feet high, was plunging down into the devoted valley.

For an instant they were unable to comprehend even the nature of the catastrophe. The reservoir was directly over their heads; the bursting of its wall they had imagined would naturally bring down the water in a dozen trickling streams or falls over the cliff above them and along the flanks of the mountain. But that its suddenly liberated volume should overflow the upland beyond and then descend in a pent-up flood by their own trail and their only avenue of escape, had been beyond their wildest fancy.

They met this smiting truth with that characteristic short laugh with which the American usually receives the blow of Fate or the unexpected—as if he recognized only the absurdity of the situation. Then they ran to the women, collected them together, and dragged them to vantages of fancied security among the bushes which flounced the long skirts of the mountain walls. But I leave this part of the description to the characteristic language of one of the party:—

"When the flood struck us, it did not seem to take any stock of us in particular, but laid itself out to 'go for' that picnic for all it was worth! It wiped it off the face of the earth in about twenty-five seconds! It first made a clean break from stem to stern, carrying everything along with it. The first thing I saw was old Judge Piper, puttin' on his best licks to get away from a big can of strawberry ice cream that was trundling after him and trying to empty itself on his collar, whenever a bigger wave lifted it. He was followed by what was left of the brass band; the big drum just humpin' itself to keep abreast o' the ice cream, mixed up with camp-stools, music-stands, a few Chinamen, and then what they call in them big San Francisco processions 'citizens generally.' The hull thing swept up the canyon inside o' thirty seconds. Then, what Captain Fairfax called 'the reflex action in the laws o' motion' happened, and darned if the hull blamed procession didn't sweep back again—this time all the heavy artillery, such as camp-kettles, lager beer kegs, bottles, glasses, and crockery that was left behind takin' the lead now, and Judge Piper and that ice cream can bringin' up the rear. As the jedge passed us the second time, we noticed that that ice cream can— hevin' swallowed water—was kinder losing its wind, and we encouraged the old man by shoutin' out, 'Five to one on him!' And then, you wouldn't believe what followed. Why, darn my skin, when that 'reflex' met the current at the other end, it just swirled around again in what Captain Fairfax called the 'centrifugal curve,' and just went round and round the canyon like ez when yer washin' the dirt out o' a prospectin' pan— every now and then washin' some one of the boys that was in it, like scum, up ag'in the banks.

"We managed in this way to snake out the judge, jest ez he was sailin' round on the home stretch, passin' the quarter post two lengths ahead o' the can. A good deal o' the ice cream had washed away, but it took us ten minutes to shake the cracked ice and powdered salt out o' the old man's clothes, and warm him up again in the laurel bush where he was clinging. This sort o' 'Here we go round the mulberry bush' kep' on until most o' the humans was got out, and only the furniture o' the picnic was left in the race. Then it got kinder mixed up, and went sloshin' round here and there, ez the water kep' comin' down by the trail. Then Lulu Piper, what I was holdin' up all the time in a laurel bush, gets an idea, for all she was wet and draggled; and ez the things went bobbin' round, she calls out the figures o' a cotillon to 'em. 'Two camp-stools forward.' 'Sashay and back to your places.' 'Change partners.' 'Hands all round.'"

"She was clear grit, you bet! And the joke caught on and the other girls jined in, and it kinder cheered 'em, for they was wantin' it. Then Fludder allowed to pacify 'em by sayin' he just figured up the size o' the reservoir and the size o' the canyon, and he kalkilated that the cube was about ekal, and the canyon couldn't flood any more. And then Lulu—who was peart as a jay and couldn't be fooled—speaks up and says, 'What's the matter with the ditch, Dick?'"

"Lord! then we knew that she knew the worst; for of course all the water in the ditch itself—fifty miles of it!—was drainin' now into that reservoir and was bound to come down to the canyon."

It was at this point that the situation became really desperate, for they had now crawled up the steep sides as far as the bushes afforded foothold, and the water was still rising. The chatter of the girls ceased, there were long silences, in which the men discussed the wildest plans, and proposed to tear their shirts into strips to make ropes to support the girls by sticks driven into the mountain side. It was in one of those intervals that the distinct strokes of a woodman's axe were heard high on the upland at the point where the trail descended to the canyon. Every ear was alert, but only those on one side of the canyon could get a fair view of the spot. This was the good fortune of Captain Fairfax and Georgy Piper, who had climbed to the highest bush on that side, and were now standing up, gazing excitedly in that direction.

"Some one is cutting down a tree at the head of the trail," shouted Fairfax. The response and joyful explanation, "for a dam across the trail," was on everybody's lips at the same time.

But the strokes of the axe were slow and painfully inter-mittent. Impatience burst out.

"Yell to him to hurry up! Why haven't they brought two men?"

"It's only one man," shouted the captain, "and he seems to be a cripple. By Jiminy!—it is—yes!—it's Tom Sparrell!"

There was a dead silence. Then, I grieve to say, shame and its twin brother rage took possession of their weak humanity. Oh, yes! It was all of a piece! Why in the name of Folly hadn't he sent for an able-bodied man. Were they to be drowned through his cranky obstinacy?

The blows still went on slowly. Presently, however, they seemed to alternate with other blows—but alas! they were slower, and if possible feebler!

"Have they got another cripple to work?" roared the Contingent in one furious voice.

"No—it's a woman—a little one—yes! a girl. Hello! Why, sure as you live, it's Delaware!"

A spontaneous cheer burst from the Contingent, partly as a rebuke to Sparrell, I think, partly from some shame over their previous rage. He could take it as he liked.

Still the blows went on distressingly slow. The girls were hoisted on the men's shoulders; the men were half submerged. Then there was a painful pause; then a crumbling crash. Another cheer went up from the canyon.

"It's down! straight across the trail," shouted Fairfax, "and a part of the bank on the top of it."

There was another moment of suspense. Would it hold or be carried away by the momentum of the flood? It held! In a few moments Fairfax again gave voice to the cheering news that the flow had stopped and the submerged trail was reappearing. In twenty minutes it was clear—a muddy river bed, but possible of ascent! Of course there was no diminution of the water in the canyon, which had no outlet, yet it now was possible for the party to swing from bush to bush along the mountain side until the foot of the trail—no longer an opposing one—was reached. There were some missteps and mishaps,—flounderings in the water, and some dangerous rescues,—but in half an hour the whole concourse stood upon the trail and commenced the ascent. It was a slow, difficult, and lugubrious procession—I fear not the best-tempered one, now that the stimulus of danger and chivalry was past. When they reached the dam made by the fallen tree, although they were obliged to make a long detour to avoid its steep sides, they could see how successfully it had diverted the current to a declivity on the other side.

But strangely enough they were greeted by nothing else! Sparrell and the youngest Miss Piper were gone; and when they at last reached the highroad, they were astounded to hear from a passing teamster that no one in the settlement knew anything of the disaster!

This was the last drop in their cup of bitterness! They who had expected that the settlement was waiting breathlessly for their rescue, who anticipated that they would be welcomed as heroes, were obliged to meet the ill-concealed amusement of passengers and friends at their dishevelled and bedraggled appearance, which suggested only the blundering mishaps of an ordinary summer outing! "Boatin' in the reservoir, and fell in?" "Playing at canal-boat in the Ditch?" were some of the cheerful hypotheses. The fleeting sense of gratitude they had felt for their deliverers was dissipated by the time they had reached their homes, and their rancor increased by the information that when the earthquake occurred Mr. Tom Sparrell and Miss Delaware were enjoying a "pasear" in the forest—he having a half-holiday by virtue of the festival—and that the earthquake had revived his fears of a catastrophe. The two had procured axes in the woodman's hut and did what they thought was necessary to relieve the situation of the picnickers. But the very modesty of this account of their own performance had the effect of belittling the catastrophe itself, and the picnickers' report of their exceeding peril was received with incredulous laughter.

For the first time in the history of Red Gulch there was a serious division between the Piper family, supported by the Contingent, and the rest of the settlement. Tom Sparrell's warning was remembered by the latter, and the ingratitude of the picnickers to their rescuers commented upon; the actual calamity to the reservoir was more or less attributed to the imprudent and reckless contiguity of the revelers on that day, and there were not wanting those who referred the accident itself to the machinations of the scheming Ditch Director Piper!

It was said that there was a stormy scene in the Piper household that evening. The judge had demanded that Delaware should break off her acquaintance with Sparrell, and she had refused; the judge had demanded of Sparrell's employer that he should discharge him, and had been met with the astounding information that Sparrell was already a silent partner in the concern. At this revelation Judge Piper was alarmed; while he might object to a clerk who could not support a wife, as a consistent democrat he could not oppose a fairly prosperous tradesman. A final appeal was made to Delaware; she was implored to consider the situation of her sisters, who had all made more ambitious marriages or were about to make them. Why should she now degrade the family by marrying a country storekeeper?

It is said that here the youngest Miss Piper made a memorable reply, and a revelation the truth of which was never gainsaid:—

"You all wanter know why I'm going to marry Tom Sparrell?" she queried, standing up and facing the whole family circle.

"Yes."

"Why I prefer him to the hull caboodle that you girls have married or are going to marry?" she continued, meditatively biting the end of her braid.

"Yes."

"Well, he's the only man of the whole lot that hasn't proposed to me first."

It is presumed that Sparrell made good the omission, or that the family were glad to get rid of her, for they were married that autumn. And really a later comparison of the family records shows that while Captain Fairfax remained "Captain Fairfax," and the other sons-in-law did not advance proportionately in standing or riches, the lame storekeeper of Red Gulch became the Hon. Senator Tom Sparrell.

A WIDOW OF THE SANTA ANA VALLEY

The Widow Wade was standing at her bedroom window staring out, in that vague instinct which compels humanity in moments of doubt and perplexity to seek this change of observation or superior illumination. Not that Mrs. Wade's disturbance was of a serious character. She had passed the acute stage of widowhood by at least two years, and the slight redness of her soft eyelids as well as the droop of her pretty mouth were merely the recognized outward and visible signs of the grievously minded religious community in which she lived. The mourning she still wore was also partly in conformity with the sad-colored garments of her neighbors, and the necessities of the rainy season. She was in comfortable circumstances, the mistress of a large ranch in the valley, which had lately become more valuable by the extension of a wagon road through its centre. She was simply worrying whether she should go to a "sociable" ending with "a dance"—a daring innovation of some strangers—at the new hotel, or continue to eschew such follies, that were, according to local belief, unsuited to "a vale of tears."

Indeed at this moment the prospect she gazed abstractedly upon seemed to justify that lugubrious description. The Santa Ana Valley—a long monotonous level—was dimly visible through moving curtains of rain or veils of mist, to the black mourning edge of the horizon, and had looked like that for months. The valley—in some remote epoch an arm of the San Francisco Bay—every rainy season seemed to be trying to revert to its original condition, and, long after the early spring had laid on its liberal color in strips, bands, and patches of blue and yellow, the blossoms of mustard and lupine glistened like wet paint. Nevertheless on that rich alluvial soil Nature's tears seemed only to fatten the widow's acres and increase her crops. Her neighbors, too, were equally prosperous. Yet for six months of the year the recognized expression of Santa Ana was one of sadness, and for the other six months—of resignation. Mrs. Wade had yielded early to this influence, as she had to others, in the weakness of her gentle nature, and partly as it was more becoming the singular tragedy that had made her a widow.

The late Mr. Wade had been found dead with a bullet through his head in a secluded part of the road over Heavy Tree Hill in Sonora County. Near him lay two other bodies, one afterwards identified as John Stubbs, a resident of the Hill, and probably a traveling companion of Wade's, and the other a noted desperado and highwayman, still masked, as at the moment of the attack. Wade and his companion had probably sold their lives dearly, and against odds, for another mask was found on the ground, indicating that the attack was not single-handed, and as Wade's body had not yet been rifled, it was evident that the remaining highwayman had fled in haste. The hue and cry had been given by apparently the only one of the travelers who escaped, but as he was hastening to take the overland coach to the East at the time, his testimony could not be submitted to the coroner's deliberation. The facts, however, were sufficiently plain for a verdict of willful murder against the highwayman, although it was believed that the absent witness had basely deserted his companion and left him to his fate, or, as was suggested by others, that he might even have been an accomplice. It was this circumstance which protracted comment on the incident, and the sufferings of the widow, far beyond that rapid obliteration which usually overtook such affairs in the feverish haste of the early days. It caused her to remove to Santa Ana, where her old father had feebly ranched a "quarter section" in the valley. He survived her husband only a few months, leaving her the property, and once more in mourning. Perhaps this continuity of woe endeared her to a neighborhood where distinctive ravages of diphtheria or scarlet fever gave a kind of social preeminence to any household, and she was so sympathetically assisted by her neighbors in the management of the ranch that, from an unkempt and wasteful wilderness, it became paying property. The slim, willowy figure, soft red-lidded eyes, and deep crape of "Sister Wade" at church or prayer-meeting was grateful to the soul of these gloomy worshipers, and in time she herself found that the arm of these dyspeptics of mind and body was nevertheless strong and sustaining. Small wonder that she should hesitate to-night about plunging into inconsistent, even though trifling, frivolities.

But apart from this superficial reason, there was another instinctive one deep down in the recesses of Mrs. Wade's timid heart which she had kept to herself, and indeed would have tearfully resented had it been offered by another. The late Mr. Wade had been, in fact, a singular example of this kind of frivolous existence carried to a man-like excess. Besides being a patron of amusements, Mr. Wade gambled, raced, and drank. He was often home late, and sometimes not at all. Not that this conduct was exceptional in the "roaring days" of Heavy Tree Hill, but it had given Mrs. Wade perhaps an undue preference for a less certain, even if a more serious life. His tragic death was, of course, a kind of martyrdom, which exalted him in the feminine mind to a saintly memory; yet Mrs. Wade was not without a certain relief in that. It was voiced, perhaps crudely, by the widow of Abner Drake in a visit of condolence to the tearful Mrs.

Wade a few days after Wade's death. "It's a vale o' sorrow, Mrs. Wade," said the sympathizer, "but it has its ups and downs, and I recken ye'll be feelin' soon pretty much as I did about Abner when HE was took. It was mighty soothin' and comfortin' to feel that whatever might happen now, I always knew just whar Abner was passin' his nights." Poor slim Mrs. Wade had no disquieting sense of humor to interfere with her reception of this large truth, and she accepted it with a burst of reminiscent tears.

A long volleying shower had just passed down the level landscape, and was followed by a rolling mist from the warm saturated soil like the smoke of the discharge. Through it she could see a faint lightening of the hidden sun, again darkening through a sudden onset of rain, and changing as with her conflicting doubts and resolutions. Thus gazing, she was vaguely conscious of an addition to the landscape in the shape of a man who was passing down the road with a pack on his back like the tramping "prospectors" she had often seen at Heavy Tree Hill. That memory apparently settled her vacillating mind; she determined she would NOT go to the dance. But as she was turning away from the window a second figure, a horseman, appeared in another direction by a cross-road, a shorter cut through her domain. This she had no difficulty in recognizing as one of the strangers who were getting up the dance. She had noticed him at church on the previous Sunday. As he passed the house he appeared to be gazing at it so earnestly that she drew back from the window lest she should be seen. And then, for no reason whatever, she changed her mind once more, and resolved to go to the dance. Gravely announcing this fact to the wife of her superintendent who kept house with her in her loneliness, she thought nothing more about it. She should go in her mourning, with perhaps the addition of a white collar and frill.

It was evident, however, that Santa Ana thought a good deal

more than she did of this new idea, which seemed a part of the innovation already begun by the building up of the new hotel. It was argued by some that as the new church and new schoolhouse had been opened by prayer, it was only natural that a lighter festivity should inaugurate the opening of the hotel. "I reckon that dancin' is about the next thing to travelin' for gettin' up an appetite for refreshments, and that's what the landlord is kalkilatin' to sarve," was the remark of a gloomy but practical citizen on the veranda of "The Valley Emporium." "That's so," rejoined a bystander; "and I notice on that last box o' pills I got for chills the directions say that a little 'agreeable exercise'—not too violent—is a great assistance to the working o' the pills."

"I reckon that that Mr. Brooks who's down here lookin' arter mill property, got up the dance. He's bin round town canvassin' all the women folks and drummin' up likely gals for it. They say he actooally sent an invite to the Widder Wade," remarked another lounger. "Gosh! he's got cheek!"

"Well, gentlemen," said the proprietor judicially, "while we don't intend to hev any minin' camp fandangos or 'Frisco falals round Santa Any—(Santa Ana was proud of its simple agricultural virtues)—I ain't so hard-shelled as not to give new things a fair trial. And, after all, it's the women folk that has the say about it. Why, there's old Miss Ford sez she hasn't kicked a fut sence she left Mizoori, but wouldn't mind trying it agin. Ez to Brooks takin' that trouble—well, I suppose it's along o' his bein' HEALTHY!" He heaved a deep dyspeptic sigh, which was faintly echoed by the others. "Why, look at him now, ridin' round on that black hoss o' his, in the wet since daylight and not carin' for blind chills or rhumatiz!"

He was looking at a serape-draped horseman, the one the widow had seen on the previous night, who was now cantering slowly up the street. Seeing the group on the veranda, he rode up, threw himself lightly from his saddle, and joined them. He was an alert, determined, good-looking fellow of about thirty-five, whose smooth, smiling face hardly commended itself to Santa Ana, though his eyes were distinctly sympathetic. He glanced at the depressed group around him and became ominously serious.

"When did it happen?" he asked gravely.

"What happen?" said the nearest bystander.

"The Funeral, Flood, Fight, or Fire. Which of the four F's was it?"

"What are ye talkin' about?" said the proprietor stiffly, scenting some dangerous humor.

"YOU," said Brooks promptly. "You're all standing here, croaking like crows, this fine morning. I passed YOUR farm, Johnson, not an hour ago; the wheat just climbing out of the black adobe mud as thick as rows of pins on paper—what have YOU to grumble at? I saw YOUR stock, Briggs, over on Two-Mile Bottom, waddling along, fat as the adobe they were sticking in, their coats shining like fresh paint—what's the matter with YOU? And," turning to the proprietor, "there's YOUR shed, Saunders, over on the creek, just bursting with last year's grain that you know has gone up two hundred per cent. since you bought it at a bargain—what are YOU growling at? It's enough to provoke a fire or a famine to hear you groaning—and take care it don't, some day, as a lesson to you."

All this was so perfectly true of the prosperous burghers that they could not for a moment reply. But Briggs had recourse to what he believed to be a retaliatory taunt.

"I heard you've been askin' Widow Wade to come to your dance," he said, with a wink at the others. "Of course she said 'Yes.'"

"Of course she did," returned Brooks coolly. "I've just got her note."

"What?" ejaculated the three men together. "Mrs. Wade comin'?"

"Certainly! Why shouldn't she? And it would do YOU good to come too, and shake the limp dampness out o' you," returned Brooks, as he quietly remounted his horse and cantered away.

"Darned ef I don't think he's got his eye on the widder," said Johnson faintly.

"Or the quarter section," added Briggs gloomily.

For all that, the eventful evening came, with many lights in the staring, undraped windows of the hotel, coldly bright bunting on the still damp walls of the long dining-room, and a gentle downpour from the hidden skies above. A close carryall was especially selected to bring Mrs. Wade and her housekeeper. The widow arrived, looking a little slimmer than usual in her closely buttoned black dress, white collar and cuffs, very glistening in eye and in hair,—whose glossy black ringlets were perhaps more elaborately arranged than was her custom,—and with a faint coming and going of color, due perhaps to her agitation at this tentative reentering into worldly life, which was nevertheless quite virginal in effect. A vague solemnity pervaded the introductory proceedings, and a singular want of sociability was visible in the "sociable" part of the entertainment. People talked in whispers or with that grave precision which indicates good manners in rural communities; conversed painfully with other people whom they did not want to talk to rather than appear to be alone, or rushed aimlessly together like water drops, and then floated in broken, adherent masses over the floor. The widow became a helpless, religious centre of deacons and Sunday-school teachers, which Brooks, untiring, yet fruitless, in his attempt to produce gayety, tried in vain to break. To this gloom the untried dangers of the impending dance, duly prefigured by a lonely cottage piano and two violins in a desert of expanse, added a nervous chill. When at last the music struck up—somewhat hesitatingly and protestingly, from the circumstance that the player was the church organist, and fumbled mechanically for his stops, the attempt to make up a cotillon set was left to the heroic Brooks. Yet he barely escaped disaster when, in posing the couples, he incautiously begged them to look a little less as if they were waiting for the coffin to be borne down the aisle between them, and was rewarded by a burst of tears from Mrs. Johnson, who had lost a child two years before, and who had to be led away, while her place in the set was taken by another. Yet the cotillon passed off; a Spanish dance succeeded; "Moneymusk," with the Virginia Reel, put a slight intoxicating vibration into the air, and healthy youth at last asserted itself in a score of freckled but buxom girls in white muslin, with romping figures and laughter, at the lower end of the room. Still a rigid decorum reigned among the elder dancers, and the figures were called out in grave formality, as if, to Brooks's fancy, they were hymns given from the pulpit, until at the close of the set, in half-real, half-mock despair, he turned desperately to Mrs. Wade, his partner:—

"Do you waltz?"

Mrs. Wade hesitated. She HAD, before marriage, and was a good waltzer. "I do," she said timidly, "but do you think they"—

But before the poor widow could formulate her fears as to the reception of "round dances," Brooks had darted to the piano, and the next moment she heard with a "fearful joy" the opening bars of a waltz. It was an old Julien waltz, fresh still in the fifties, daring, provocative to foot, swamping to intellect, arresting to judgment, irresistible, supreme! Before Mrs. Wade could protest, Brooks's arm had gathered up her slim figure, and with one quick backward sweep and swirl they were off! The floor was cleared for them in a sudden bewilderment of alarm—a suspense of burning curiosity. The widow's little feet tripped quickly, her long black skirt swung out; as she turned the corner there was not only a sudden revelation of her pretty ankles, but, what was more startling, a dazzling flash of frilled and laced petticoat, which at once convinced every woman in the room that the act had been premeditated for days! Yet even that criticism was presently forgotten in the pervading intoxication of the music and the movement. The younger people fell into it with wild rompings, whirlings, and clasping of hands and waists. And stranger than all, a corybantic enthusiasm seized upon the emotionally religious, and those priests and priestesses of Cybele who were famous for their frenzy and passion in camp-meeting devotions seemed to find an equal expression that night in the waltz. And when, flushed and panting, Mrs. Wade at last halted on the arm of her partner, they were nearly knocked over by the revolving Johnson and Mrs. Stubbs in a whirl of gloomy exultation! Deacons and Sunday-school teachers waltzed together until the long room shook, and the very bunting on the walls waved and fluttered with the gyrations of those religious dervishes. Nobody knew—nobody cared how long this frenzy lasted—it ceased only with the collapse of the musicians. Then, with much vague bewilderment, inward trepidation, awkward and incoherent partings, everybody went dazedly home; there was no other dancing after that—the waltz was the one event of the festival and of the history of Santa Ana. And later that night, when the timid Mrs. Wade, in the seclusion of her own room and the disrobing of her slim figure, glanced at her spotless frilled and laced petticoat lying on a chair, a faint smile—the first of her widowhood—curved the corners of her pretty mouth.

A week of ominous silence regarding the festival succeeded in Santa Ana. The local paper gave the fullest particulars of the opening of the hotel, but contented itself with saying: "The entertainment concluded with a dance." Mr. Brooks, who felt himself compelled to call upon his late charming partner twice during the week, characteristically soothed her anxieties as to the result. "The fact of it is, Mrs. Wade, there's really nobody in particular to blame—and that's what gets them. They're all mixed up in it, deacons and Sunday-school teachers; and when old Johnson tried to be nasty the other evening and hoped you hadn't suffered from your exertions that night, I told him you hadn't quite recovered yet from the physical shock of having been run into by him and Mrs. Stubbs, but that, you being a lady, you didn't tell just how you felt at the exhibition he and she made of themselves. That shut him up."

"But you shouldn't have said that," said Mrs. Wade with a frightened little smile.

"No matter," returned Brooks cheerfully. "I'll take the blame of it with the others. You see they'll have to have a scapegoat—and I'm just the man, for I got up the dance! And as I'm going away, I suppose I shall bear off the sin with me into the wilderness."

"You're going away?" repeated Mrs. Wade in more genuine concern.

"Not for long," returned Brooks laughingly. "I came here to

look up a mill site, and I've found it. Meantime I think I've opened their eyes."

"You have opened mine," said the widow with timid frankness.

They were soft pretty eyes when opened, in spite of their heavy red lids, and Mr. Brooks thought that Santa Ana would be no worse if they remained open. Possibly he looked it, for Mrs. Wade said hurriedly, "I mean—that is—I've been thinking that life needn't ALWAYS be as gloomy as we make it here. And even HERE, you know, Mr. Brooks, we have six months' sunshine—though we always forget it in the rainy season."

"That's so," said Brooks cheerfully. "I once lost a heap of money through my own foolishness, and I've managed to forget it, and I even reckon to get it back again out of Santa Ana if my mill speculation holds good. So good-by, Mrs. Wade—but not for long." He shook her hand frankly and departed, leaving the widow conscious of a certain sympathetic confidence and a little grateful for—she knew not what.

This feeling remained with her most of the afternoon, and even imparted a certain gayety to her spirits, to the extent of causing her to hum softly to herself; the air being oddly enough the Julien Waltz. And when, later in the day, the shadows were closing in with the rain, word was brought to her that a stranger wished to see her in the sitting-room, she carried a less mournful mind to this function of her existence. For Mrs. Wade was accustomed to give audience to traveling agents, tradesmen, working-hands and servants, as chatelaine of her ranch, and the occasion was not novel. Yet on entering the room, which she used partly as an office, she found some difficulty in classifying the stranger, who at first glance reminded her of the tramping miner she had seen that night from her window. He was rather incongruously dressed, some articles of his apparel being finer than others; he wore a diamond pin in a scarf folded over a rough "hickory" shirt; his light trousers were tucked in common mining boots that bore stains of travel and a suggestion that he had slept in his clothes. What she could see of his unshaven face in that uncertain light expressed a kind of dogged concentration, overlaid by an assumption of ease. He got up as she came in, and with a slight "How do, ma'am," shut the door behind her and glanced furtively around the room.

"What I've got to say to ye, Mrs. Wade,—as I reckon you be,—is strictly private and confidential! Why, ye'll see afore I get through. But I thought I might just as well caution ye agin our being disturbed."

Overcoming a slight instinct of repulsion, Mrs. Wade returned, "You can speak to me here; no one will interrupt you—unless I call them," she added with a little feminine caution.

"And I reckon ye won't do that," he said with a grim smile. "You are the widow o' Pulaski Wade, late o' Heavy Tree Hill, I reckon?"

"I am," said Mrs. Wade.

"And your husband's buried up thar in the graveyard, with a monument over him setting forth his virtues ez a Christian and a square man and a high-minded citizen? And that he was foully murdered by highwaymen?"

"Yes," said Mrs. Wade, "that is the inscription."

Bret Harte

"Well, ma'am, a bigger pack o' lies never was cut on stone!"

Mrs. Wade rose, half in indignation, half in terror.

"Keep your sittin'," said the stranger, with a warning wave of his hand. "Wait till I'm through, and then you call in the hull State o' Californy, ef ye want."

The stranger's manner was so doggedly confident that Mrs. Wade sank back tremblingly in her chair. The man put his slouch hat on his knee, twirled it round once or twice, and then said with the same stubborn deliberation:—

"The highwayman in that business was your husband— Pulaski Wade—and his gang, and he was killed by one o' the men he was robbin'. Ye see, ma'am, it used to be your husband's little game to rope in three or four strangers in a poker deal at Spanish Jim's saloon—I see you've heard o' the place," he interpolated as Mrs. Wade drew back suddenly— "and when he couldn't clean 'em out in that way, or they showed a little more money than they played, he'd lay for 'em with his gang in a lone part of the trail, and go through them like any road agent. That's what he did that night—and that's how he got killed."

"How do you know this?" said Mrs. Wade, with quivering lips.

"I was one o' the men he went through before he was killed. And I'd hev got my money back, but the rest o' the gang came up, and I got away jest in time to save my life and nothin' else. Ye might remember thar was one man got away and giv' the alarm, but he was goin' on to the States by the overland coach that night and couldn't stay to be a witness. I was that man. I had paid my passage through, and I couldn't lose THAT too with my other money, so I went."

Mrs. Wade sat stunned. She remembered the missing witness, and how she had longed to see the man who was last with her husband; she remembered Spanish Jim's saloon—his well-known haunt; his frequent and unaccountable absences, the sudden influx of money which he always said he had won at cards; the diamond ring he had given her as the result of "a bet;" the forgotten recurrence of other robberies by a secret masked gang; a hundred other things that had worried her, instinctively, vaguely. She knew now, too, the meaning of the unrest that had driven her from Heavy Tree Hill—the strange unformulated fears that had haunted her even here. Yet with all this she felt, too, her present weakness—knew that this man had taken her at a disadvantage, that she ought to indignantly assert herself, deny everything, demand proof, and brand him a slanderer!

"How did—you—know it was my husband?" she stammered.

"His mask fell off in the fight; you know another mask was found—it was HIS. I saw him as plainly as I see him there!" he pointed to a daguerreotype of her husband which stood upon her desk.

Mrs. Wade could only stare vacantly, hopelessly. After a pause the man continued in a less aggressive manner and more confidential tone, which, however, only increased her terror. "I ain't sayin' that YOU knowed anything about this, ma'am, and whatever other folks might say when THEY know of it, I'll allers say that you didn't."

"What, then, did you come here for?" said the widow desperately.

"What do I come here for?" repeated the man grimly, looking around the room; "what did I come to this yer comfortable home—this yer big ranch and to a rich woman like yourself for? Well, Mrs. Wade, I come to get the six hundred dollars your husband robbed me of, that's all! I ain't askin' more! I ain't askin' interest! I ain't askin' compensation for havin' to run for my life—and," again looking grimly round the walls, "I ain't askin' more than you will give—or is my rights."

"But this house never was his; it was my father's," gasped Mrs. Wade; "you have no right"—

"Mebbe 'yes' and mebbe 'no,' Mrs. Wade," interrupted the man, with a wave of his hat; "but how about them two checks to bearer for two hundred dollars each found among your husband's effects, and collected by your lawyer for you—MY CHECKS, Mrs. Wade?"

A wave of dreadful recollection overwhelmed her. She remembered the checks found upon her husband's body, known only to her and her lawyer, believed to be gambling gains, and collected at once under his legal advice. Yet she made one more desperate effort in spite of the instinct that told her he was speaking the truth.

"But you shall have to prove it—before witnesses."

"Do you WANT me to prove it before witnesses?" said the man, coming nearer her. "Do you want to take my word and keep it between ourselves, or do you want to call in your superintendent and his men, and all Santy Any, to hear me prove your husband was a highwayman, thief, and murderer? Do you want to knock over that monument on Heavy Tree Hill, and upset your standing here among the deacons and elders? Do you want to do all this and be forced, even by your neighbors, to pay me in the end, as you will? Ef you do, call in your witnesses now and let's have it over. Mebbe it would look better ef I got the money out of YOUR FRIENDS than ye—a woman! P'raps you're right!"

He made a step towards the door, but she stopped him.

"No! no! wait! It's a large sum—I haven't it with me," she stammered, thoroughly beaten.

"Ye kin get it."

"Give me time!" she implored. "Look! I'll give you a hundred down now,—all I have here,—the rest another time!" She nervously opened a drawer of her desk and taking out a buckskin bag of gold thrust it in his hand. "There! go away now!" She lifted her thin hands despairingly to her head. "Go! do!"

The man seemed struck by her manner. "I don't want to be hard on a woman," he said slowly. "I'll go now and come back again at nine to-night. You can git the money, or what's as good, a check to bearer, by then. And ef ye'll take my advice, you won't ask no advice from others, ef you want to keep your secret. Just now it's safe with me; I'm a square man, ef I seem to be a hard one." He made a gesture as if to take her hand, but as she drew shrinkingly away, he changed it to an awkward bow, and the next moment was gone.

She started to her feet, but the unwonted strain upon her nerves and frail body had been greater than she knew. She made a step forward, felt the room whirl round her and then seem to collapse beneath her feet, and, clutching at her chair, sank back into it, fainting.

How long she lay there she never knew. She was at last conscious of some one bending over her, and a voice—the voice of Mr. Brooks—in her ear, saying, "I beg your pardon;

you seem ill. Shall I call some one?"

"No!" she gasped, quickly recovering herself with an effort, and staring round her. "Where is—when did you come in?"

"Only this moment. I was leaving tonight, sooner than I expected, and thought I'd say good-by. They told me that you had been engaged with a stranger, but he had just gone. I beg your pardon—I see you are ill. I won't detain you any longer."

"No! no! don't go! I am better—better," she said feverishly. As she glanced at his strong and sympathetic face a wild idea seized her. He was a stranger here, an alien to these people, like herself. The advice that she dare not seek from others, from her half-estranged religious friends, from even her superintendent and his wife, dare she ask from him? Perhaps he saw this frightened doubt, this imploring appeal, in her eyes, for he said gently, "Is it anything I can do for you?"

"Yes," she said, with the sudden desperation of weakness; "I want you to keep a secret."

"Yours?—yes!" he said promptly.

Whereat poor Mrs. Wade instantly burst into tears. Then, amidst her sobs, she told him of the stranger's visit, of his terrible accusations, of his demands, his expected return, and her own utter helplessness. To her terror, as she went on she saw a singular change in his kind face; he was following her with hard, eager intensity. She had half hoped, even through her fateful instincts, that he might have laughed, manlike, at her fears, or pooh-poohed the whole thing. But he did not. "You say he positively recognized your husband?" he repeated quickly.

"Yes, yes!" sobbed the widow, "and knew that daguerreotype!" she pointed to the desk.

Brooks turned quickly in that direction. Luckily his back was towards her, and she could not see his face, and the quick, startled look that came into his eyes. But when they again met hers, it was gone, and even their eager intensity had changed to a gentle commiseration. "You have only his word for it, Mrs. Wade," he said gently, "and in telling your secret to another, you have shorn the rascal of half his power over you. And he knew it. Now, dismiss the matter from your mind and leave it all to me. I will be here a few minutes before nine—AND ALONE IN THIS ROOM. Let your visitor be shown in here, and don't let us be disturbed. Don't be alarmed," he added with a faint twinkle in his eye, "there will be no fuss and no exposure!"

It lacked a few minutes of nine when Mr. Brooks was ushered into the sitting-room. As soon as he was alone he quietly examined the door and the windows, and having satisfied himself, took his seat in a chair casually placed behind the door. Presently he heard the sound of voices and a heavy footstep in the passage. He lightly felt his waistcoat pocket—it contained a pretty little weapon of power and precision, with a barrel scarcely two inches long.

The door opened, and the person outside entered the room. In an instant Brooks had shut the door and locked it behind him. The man turned fiercely, but was faced by Brooks quietly, with one finger calmly hooked in his waistcoat pocket. The man slightly recoiled from him—not as much from fear as from some vague stupefaction. "What's that for? What's your little game?" he said half contemptuously.

"No game at all," returned Brooks coolly. "You came here to sell a secret. I don't propose to have it given away first to

Bret Harte

any listener."

"YOU don't—who are YOU?"

"That's a queer question to ask of the man you are trying to personate—but I don't wonder! You're doing it d—d badly."

"Personate—YOU?" said the stranger, with staring eyes.

"Yes, ME," said Brooks quietly. "I am the only man who escaped from the robbery that night at Heavy Tree Hill and who went home by the Overland Coach."

The stranger stared, but recovered himself with a coarse laugh. "Oh, well! we're on the same lay, it appears! Both after the widow—afore we show up her husband."

"Not exactly," said Brooks, with his eyes fixed intently on the stranger. "You are here to denounce a highwayman who is DEAD and escaped justice. I am here to denounce one who is LIVING!—Stop! drop your hand; it's no use. You thought you had to deal only with a woman to-night, and your revolver isn't quite handy enough. There! down!—down! So! That'll do."

"You can't prove it," said the man hoarsely.

"Fool! In your story to that woman you have given yourself away. There were but two travelers attacked by the highwaymen. One was killed—I am the other. Where do YOU come in? What witness can you be—except as the highwayman that you are? Who is left to identify Wade but—his accomplice!"

The man's suddenly whitened face made his unshaven beard seem to bristle over his face like some wild animal's. "Well, ef you kalkilate to blow me, you've got to blow Wade and his widder too. Jest you remember that," he said whiningly.

"I've thought of that," said Brooks coolly, "and I calculate that to prevent it is worth about that hundred dollars you got from that poor woman—and no more! Now, sit down at that table, and write as I dictate."

The man looked at him in wonder, but obeyed.

"Write," said Brooks, "I hereby certify that my accusations against the late Pulaski Wade of Heavy Tree Hill are erroneous and groundless, and the result of mistaken identity, especially in regard to any complicity of his in the robbery of John Stubbs, deceased, and Henry Brooks, at Heavy Tree Hill, on the night of the 13th August, 1854."

The man looked up with a repulsive smile. "Who's the fool now, Cap'n? What's become of your hold on the widder, now?"

"Write!" said Brooks fiercely.

The sound of a pen hurriedly scratching paper followed this first outburst of the quiet Brooks.

"Sign it," said Brooks.

The man signed it.

"Now go," said Brooks, unlocking the door, "but remember, if you should ever be inclined to revisit Santa Ana, you will find ME living here also."

The man slunk out of the door and into the passage like a wild animal returning to the night and darkness. Brooks took up the paper, rejoined Mrs. Wade in the parlor, and laid it before her.

"But," said the widow, trembling even in her joy, "do you— do you think he was REALLY mistaken?"

"Positive," said Brooks coolly. "It's true, it's a mistake that has cost you a hundred dollars, but there are some mistakes that are worth that to be kept quiet."

*****

They were married a year later; but there is no record that in after years of conjugal relations with a weak, charming, but sometimes trying woman, Henry Brooks was ever tempted to tell her the whole truth of the robbery of Heavy Tree Hill.

THE MERMAID OF LIGHTHOUSE POINT

Some forty years ago, on the northern coast of California, near the Golden Gate, stood a lighthouse. Of a primitive class, since superseded by a building more in keeping with the growing magnitude of the adjacent port, it attracted little attention from the desolate shore, and, it was alleged, still less from the desolate sea beyond. A gray structure of timber, stone, and glass, it was buffeted and harried by the constant trade winds, baked by the unclouded six months' sun, lost for a few hours in the afternoon sea-fog, and laughed over by circling guillemots from the Farallones. It was kept by a recluse—a preoccupied man of scientific tastes, who, in shameless contrast to his fellow immigrants, had applied to the government for this scarcely lucrative position as a means of securing the seclusion he valued more than gold. Some believed that he was the victim of an early disappointment in love—a view charitably taken by those who also believed that the government would not have appointed "a crank" to a position of responsibility. Howbeit, he fulfilled his duties, and, with the assistance of an Indian, even cultivated a small patch of ground beside the light-house. His isolation was complete! There was little to attract wanderers here: the nearest mines were fifty miles away; the virgin forest on the mountains inland were penetrated only by sawmills and woodmen from the Bay settlements, equally remote. Although by the shore-line the lights of the great

Bret Harte

port were sometimes plainly visible, yet the solitude around him was peopled only by Indians,—a branch of the great northern tribe of "root-diggers,"—peaceful and simple in their habits, as yet undisturbed by the white man, nor stirred into antagonism by aggression. Civilization only touched him at stated intervals, and then by the more expeditious sea from the government boat that brought him supplies. But for his contiguity to the perpetual turmoil of wind and sea, he might have passed a restful Arcadian life in his surroundings; for even his solitude was sometimes haunted by this faint reminder of the great port hard by that pulsated with an equal unrest. Nevertheless, the sands before his door and the rocks behind him seemed to have been untrodden by any other white man's foot since their upheaval from the ocean. It was true that the little bay beside him was marked on the map as "Sir Francis Drake's Bay," tradition having located it as the spot where that ingenious pirate and empire-maker had once landed his vessels and scraped the barnacles from his adventurous keels. But of this Edgar Pomfrey—or "Captain Pomfrey," as he was called by virtue of his half-nautical office—had thought little.

For the first six months he had thoroughly enjoyed his seclusion. In the company of his books, of which he had brought such a fair store that their shelves lined his snug corners to the exclusion of more comfortable furniture, he found his principal recreation. Even his unwonted manual labor, the trimming of his lamp and cleaning of his reflectors, and his personal housekeeping, in which his Indian help at times assisted, he found a novel and interesting occupation. For outdoor exercise, a ramble on the sands, a climb to the rocky upland, or a pull in the lighthouse boat, amply sufficed him. "Crank" as he was supposed to be, he was sane enough to guard against any of those early lapses into barbarism which marked the lives of some solitary gold-miners. His own taste, as well as the duty of his office, kept his person and habitation sweet and clean, and his habits regular. Even the little cultivated patch of ground on the lee side of the tower was symmetrical and well ordered. Thus the outward light of Captain Pomfrey shone forth over the wilderness of shore and wave, even like his beacon, whatever his inward illumination may have been.

It was a bright summer morning, remarkable even in the monotonous excellence of the season, with a slight touch of warmth which the invincible Northwest Trades had not yet chilled. There was still a faint haze off the coast, as if last night's fog had been caught in the quick sunshine, and the shining sands were hot, but without the usual dazzling glare. A faint perfume from a quaint lilac-colored beach-flower, whose clustering heads dotted the sand like bits of blown spume, took the place of that smell of the sea which the odorless Pacific lacked. A few rocks, half a mile away, lifted themselves above the ebb tide at varying heights as they lay on the trough of the swell, were crested with foam by a striking surge, or cleanly erased in the full sweep of the sea. Beside, and partly upon one of the higher rocks, a singular object was moving.

Pomfrey was interested but not startled. He had once or twice seen seals disporting on these rocks, and on one occasion a sea-lion,—an estray from the familiar rocks on the other side of the Golden Gate. But he ceased work in his garden patch, and coming to his house, exchanged his hoe for a telescope. When he got the mystery in focus he suddenly stopped and rubbed the object-glass with his handkerchief. But even when he applied the glass to his eye for a second time, he could scarcely believe his eyesight. For the object seemed to be a WOMAN, the lower part of her figure submerged in the sea, her long hair depending over her shoulders and waist. There was nothing in her attitude to suggest terror or that she was the victim of some accident. She moved slowly and complacently with the sea, and even—a more staggering suggestion—appeared to be combing out the strands of her long hair with her fingers. With her body half concealed she might have been a mermaid!

He swept the foreshore and horizon with his glass; there was neither boat nor ship—nor anything that moved, except the long swell of the Pacific. She could have come only from the sea; for to reach the rocks by land she would have had to pass before the lighthouse, while the narrow strip of shore which curved northward beyond his range of view he knew was inhabited only by Indians. But the woman was unhesitatingly and appallingly WHITE, and her hair light even to a golden gleam in the sunshine.

Pomfrey was a gentleman, and as such was amazed, dismayed, and cruelly embarrassed. If she was a simple bather from some vicinity hitherto unknown and unsuspected by him, it was clearly his business to shut up his glass and go back to his garden patch—although the propinquity of himself and the lighthouse must have been as plainly visible to her as she was to him. On the other hand, if she was the survivor of some wreck and in distress—or, as he even fancied from her reckless manner, bereft of her senses, his duty to rescue her was equally clear. In his dilemma he determined upon a compromise and ran to his boat. He would pull out to sea, pass between the rocks and the curving sand-spit, and examine the sands and sea more closely for signs of wreckage, or some overlooked waiting boat near the shore. He would be within hail if she needed him, or she could escape to her boat if she had one.

In another moment his boat was lifting on the swell towards the rocks. He pulled quickly, occasionally turning to note that the strange figure, whose movements were quite discernible to the naked eye, was still there, but gazing more earnestly towards the nearest shore for any sign of life or occupation. In ten minutes he had reached the curve where the trend opened northward, and the long line of shore stretched before him. He swept it eagerly with a single searching glance. Sea and shore were empty. He turned quickly to the rock, scarcely a hundred yards on his beam. It was empty too! Forgetting his previous scruples, he pulled directly for it until his keel grated on its submerged base. There was nothing there but the rock, slippery with the yellow-green slime of seaweed and kelp—neither trace nor sign of the figure that had occupied it a moment ago. He pulled around it; there was no cleft or hiding-place. For an instant his heart leaped at the sight of something white, caught in a jagged tooth of the outlying reef, but it was only the bleached fragment of a bamboo orange-crate, cast from the deck of some South Sea trader, such as often strewed the beach. He lay off the rock, keeping way in the swell, and scrutinizing the glittering sea. At last he pulled back to the lighthouse, perplexed and discomfited.

Was it simply a sporting seal, transformed by some trick of his vision? But he had seen it through his glass, and now remembered such details as the face and features framed in their contour of golden hair, and believed he could even have identified them. He examined the rock again with his glass, and was surprised to see how clearly it was outlined now in its barren loneliness. Yet he must have been mistaken. His scientific and accurate mind allowed of no errant fancy, and he had always sneered at the marvelous as the result of hasty or superficial observation. He was a little worried at this lapse of his healthy accuracy,—fearing that it might be the result of his seclusion and loneliness,—akin to the visions of the recluse and solitary. It was strange, too, that it should take the shape of a woman; for Edgar Pomfrey had a story— the usual old and foolish one.

Then his thoughts took a lighter phase, and he turned to the memory of his books, and finally to the books themselves. From a shelf he picked out a volume of old voyages, and turned to a remembered passage: "In other seas doe abound marvells soche as Sea Spyders of the bigness of a pinnace, the wich they have been known to attack and destroy; Sea Vypers which reach to the top of a goodly maste, whereby they are able to draw marinners from the rigging by the suction of their breathes; and Devill Fyshe, which vomit fire by night which makyth the sea to shine prodigiously, and mermaydes. They are half fyshe and half mayde of grate Beauty, and have been seen of divers godly and creditable witnesses swymming beside rocks, hidden to their waist in the sea, combing of their hayres, to the help of whych they carry a small mirrore of the bigness of their fingers." Pomfrey laid the book aside with a faint smile. To even this credulity he might come!

Nevertheless, he used the telescope again that day. But there was no repetition of the incident, and he was forced to believe that he had been the victim of some extraordinary illusion. The next morning, however, with his calmer judgment doubts began to visit him. There was no one of whom he could make inquiries but his Indian helper, and their conversation had usually been restricted to the language of signs or the use of a few words he had picked up. He contrived, however, to ask if there was a "waugee" (white) woman in the neighborhood. The Indian shook his head in surprise. There was no "waugee" nearer than the remote mountain-ridge to which he pointed. Pomfrey was obliged to be content with this. Even had his vocabulary been larger, he would as soon have thought of revealing the embarrassing secret of this woman, whom he believed to be of his own race, to a mere barbarian as he would of asking him to verify his own impressions by allowing him to look at her that morning. The next day, however, something happened which forced him to resume his inquiries. He was rowing around the curving spot when he saw a number of black objects on the northern sands moving in and out of the surf, which he presently made out as Indians. A nearer approach satisfied him that they were wading squaws and children gathering seaweed and shells. He would have pushed his acquaintance still nearer, but as his boat rounded the point, with one accord they all scuttled away like frightened sandpipers. Pomfrey, on his return, asked his Indian retainer if they could swim. "Oh, yes!" "As far as the rock?" "Yes." Yet Pomfrey was not satisfied. The color of his strange apparition remained unaccounted for, and it was not that of an Indian woman.

Trifling events linger long in a monotonous existence, and it was nearly a week before Pomfrey gave up his daily telescopic inspection of the rock. Then he fell back upon his books again, and, oddly enough, upon another volume of voyages, and so chanced upon the account of Sir Francis Drake's occupation of the bay before him. He had always thought it strange that the great adventurer had left no trace or sign of his sojourn there; still stranger that he should have overlooked the presence of gold, known even to the Indians themselves, and have lost a discovery far beyond his wildest dreams and a treasure to which the cargoes of those Philippine galleons he had more or less successfully intercepted were trifles. Had the restless explorer been content to pace those dreary sands during three weeks of inactivity, with no thought of penetrating the inland forests behind the range, or of even entering the nobler bay beyond? Or was the location of the spot a mere tradition as wild and unsupported as the "marvells" of the other volume? Pomfrey had the skepticism of the scientific, inquiring mind.

Two weeks had passed and he was returning from a long climb inland, when he stopped to rest in his descent to the

Bret Harte

sea. The panorama of the shore was before him, from its uttermost limit to the lighthouse on the northern point. The sun was still one hour high, it would take him about that time to reach home. But from this coign of vantage he could see—what he had not before observed—that what he had always believed was a little cove on the northern shore was really the estuary of a small stream which rose near him and eventually descended into the ocean at that point. He could also see that beside it was a long low erection of some kind, covered with thatched brush, which looked like a "barrow," yet showed signs of habitation in the slight smoke that rose from it and drifted inland. It was not far out of his way, and he resolved to return in that direction. On his way down he once or twice heard the barking of an Indian dog, and knew that he must be in the vicinity of an encampment. A camp-fire, with the ashes yet warm, proved that he was on the trail of one of the nomadic tribes, but the declining sun warned him to hasten home to his duty. When he at last reached the estuary, he found that the building beside it was little else than a long hut, whose thatched and mud-plastered mound-like roof gave it the appearance of a cave. Its single opening and entrance abutted on the water's edge, and the smoke he had noticed rolled through this entrance from a smouldering fire within. Pomfrey had little difficulty in recognizing the purpose of this strange structure from the accounts he had heard from "loggers" of the Indian customs. The cave was a "sweat-house"—a calorific chamber in which the Indians closely shut themselves, naked, with a "smudge" or smoul-dering fire of leaves, until, perspiring and half suffocated, they rushed from the entrance and threw themselves into the water before it. The still smouldering fire told him that the house had been used that morning, and he made no doubt that the Indians were encamped near by. He would have liked to pursue his researches further, but he found he had already trespassed upon his remaining time, and he turned somewhat abruptly away—so abruptly, in fact, that a figure, which had evidently been cautiously following him at a distance, had not time to get away. His heart leaped with astonishment. It was the woman he had seen on the rock.

Although her native dress now only disclosed her head and hands, there was no doubt about her color, and it was distinctly white, save for the tanning of exposure and a slight red ochre marking on her low forehead. And her hair, long and unkempt as it was, showed that he had not erred in his first impression of it. It was a tawny flaxen, with fainter bleachings where the sun had touched it most. Her eyes were of a clear Northern blue. Her dress, which was quite distinctive in that it was neither the cast off finery of civilization nor the cheap "government" flannels and calicoes usually worn by the Californian tribes, was purely native, and of fringed deerskin, and consisted of a long, loose shirt and leggings worked with bright feathers and colored shells. A necklace, also of shells and fancy pebbles, hung round her neck. She seemed to be a fully developed woman, in spite of the girlishness of her flowing hair, and notwithstanding the shapeless length of her gaberdine-like garment, taller than the ordinary squaw.

Pomfrey saw all this in a single flash of perception, for the next instant she was gone, disappearing behind the sweat-house. He ran after her, catching sight of her again, half doubled up, in the characteristic Indian trot, dodging around rocks and low bushes as she fled along the banks of the stream. But for her distinguishing hair, she looked in her flight like an ordinary frightened squaw. This, which gave a sense of unmanliness and ridicule to his own pursuit of her, with the fact that his hour of duty was drawing near and he was still far from the lighthouse, checked him in full career, and he turned regretfully away. He had called after her at first, and she had not heeded him. What he would have said to her he did not know. He hastened home discomfited, even embarrassed—yet excited to a degree he had not deemed possible in himself.

During the morning his thoughts were full of her. Theory after theory for her strange existence there he examined and dismissed. His first thought, that she was a white woman—some settler's wife—masquerading in Indian garb, he abandoned when he saw her moving; no white woman could imitate that Indian trot, nor would remember to attempt it if she were frightened. The idea that she was a captive white, held by the Indians, became ridiculous when he thought of the nearness of civilization and the peaceful, timid character of the "digger" tribes. That she was some unfortunate demented creature who had escaped from her keeper and wandered into the wilderness, a glance at her clear, frank, intelligent, curious eyes had contradicted. There was but one theory left—the most sensible and practical one—that she was the offspring of some white man and Indian squaw. Yet this he found, oddly enough, the least palatable to his fancy. And the few half-breeds he had seen were not at all like her.

The next morning he had recourse to his Indian retainer, "Jim." With infinite difficulty, protraction, and not a little embarrassment, he finally made him understand that he had seen a "white squaw" near the "sweat-house," and that he wanted to know more about her. With equal difficulty Jim finally recognized the fact of the existence of such a person, but immediately afterwards shook his head in an emphatic negation. With greater difficulty and greater mortification Pomfrey presently ascertained that Jim's negative referred to a supposed abduction of the woman which he understood that his employer seriously contemplated. But he also learned that she was a real Indian, and that there were three or four others like her, male and female, in that vicinity; that from a "skeena mowitch" (little baby) they were all like that, and that their parents were of the same color, but never a white or "waugee" man or woman among them; that they were looked upon as a distinct and superior caste of Indians, and enjoyed certain privileges with the tribe; that they superstitiously avoided white men, of whom they had the greatest fear, and that they were protected in this by the other Indians; that it was marvelous and almost beyond belief that Pomfrey had been able to see one, for no other white man had, or was even aware of their existence.

How much of this he actually understood, how much of it was lying and due to Jim's belief that he wished to abduct the fair stranger, Pomfrey was unable to determine. There was enough, however, to excite his curiosity strongly and occupy his mind to the exclusion of his books—save one. Among his smaller volumes he had found a travel book of the "Chinook Jargon," with a lexicon of many of the words commonly used by the Northern Pacific tribes. An hour or two's trial with the astonished Jim gave him an increased vocabulary and a new occupation. Each day the incongruous pair took a lesson from the lexicon. In a week Pomfrey felt he would be able to accost the mysterious stranger. But he did not again surprise her in any of his rambles, or even in a later visit to the sweat-house. He had learned from Jim that the house was only used by the "bucks," or males, and that her appearance there had been accidental. He recalled that he had had the impression that she had been stealthily following him, and the recollection gave him a pleasure he could not account for. But an incident presently occurred which gave him a new idea of her relations towards him.

The difficulty of making Jim understand had hitherto prevented Pomfrey from intrusting him with the care of the lantern; but with the aid of the lexicon he had been able to make him comprehend its working, and under Pomfrey's personal guidance the Indian had once or twice lit the lamp and set its machinery in motion. It remained for him only to test Jim's unaided capacity, in case of his own absence or illness. It happened to be a warm, beautiful sunset, when the afternoon fog had for once delayed its invasion of the shore-line, that he left the lighthouse to Jim's undivided care, and reclining on a sand-dune still warm from the sun, lazily watched the result of Jim's first essay. As the twilight deepened, and the first flash of the lantern strove with the dying glories of the sun, Pomfrey presently became aware that he was not the only watcher. A little gray figure creeping on all fours suddenly glided out of the shadow of another sand-dune and then halted, falling back on its knees, gazing fixedly at the growing light. It was the woman he had seen. She was not a dozen yards away, and in her eagerness and utter absorption in the light had evidently overlooked him. He could see her face distinctly, her lips parted half in wonder, half with the breathless absorption of a devotee. A faint sense of disappointment came over him. It was not HIM she was watching, but the light! As it swelled out over the darkening gray sand she turned as if to watch its effect around her, and caught sight of Pomfrey. With a little startled cry—the first she had uttered—she darted away. He did not follow. A moment before, when he first saw her, an Indian salutation which he had learned from Jim had risen to his lips, but in the odd feeling which her fascination of the light had caused him he had not spoken. He watched her bent figure scuttling away like some frightened animal, with a critical consciousness that she was really scarce human, and went back to the lighthouse. He would not run after her again! Yet that evening he continued to think of her, and recalled her voice, which struck him now as having been at once melodious and childlike, and wished he had at least spoken, and perhaps elicited a reply.

He did not, however, haunt the sweat-house near the river again. Yet he still continued his lessons with Jim, and in this way, perhaps, although quite unpremeditatedly, enlisted a humble ally. A week passed in which he had not alluded to her, when one morning, as he was returning from a row, Jim met him mysteriously on the beach.

"S'pose him come slow, slow," said Jim gravely, airing his newly acquired English; "make no noise—plenty catchee Indian maiden." The last epithet was the polite lexicon equivalent of squaw.

Pomfrey, not entirely satisfied in his mind, nevertheless softly followed the noiselessly gliding Jim to the lighthouse. Here Jim cautiously opened the door, motioning Pomfrey to enter.

The base of the tower was composed of two living rooms, a storeroom and oil-tank. As Pomfrey entered, Jim closed the door softly behind him. The abrupt transition from the glare of the sands and sun to the semi-darkness of the storeroom at first prevented him from seeing anything, but he was instantly distracted by a scurrying flutter and wild beating of the walls, as of a caged bird. In another moment he could make out the fair stranger, quivering with excitement, passionately dashing at the barred window, the walls, the locked door, and circling around the room in her desperate attempt to find an egress, like a captured seagull. Amazed, mystified, indignant with Jim, himself, and even his unfortunate captive, Pomfrey called to her in Chinook to stop, and going to the door, flung it wide open. She darted by him, raising her soft blue eyes for an instant in a swift, sidelong glance of half appeal, half-frightened admiration, and rushed out into the open. But here, to his surprise, she did not run away. On the contrary, she drew herself up with a dignity that seemed to increase her height, and walked majestically towards Jim, who at her unexpected exit had suddenly thrown himself upon the sand, in utterly abject terror and supplication. She approached him slowly, with one small hand uplifted in a menacing gesture. The man writhed and squirmed before her. Then she turned, caught sight of Pomfrey standing in the doorway, and walked quietly away. Amazed, yet gratified with this new assertion of herself, Pomfrey respectfully, but alas! incautiously, called after her. In an instant, at the sound of his voice, she dropped again into her slouching Indian trot and glided away over the sandhills.

Pomfrey did not add any reproof of his own to the discomfiture of his Indian retainer. Neither did he attempt to inquire the secret of this savage girl's power over him. It was evident he had spoken truly when he told his master that she was of a superior caste. Pomfrey recalled her erect and indignant figure standing over the prostrate Jim, and was again perplexed and disappointed at her sudden lapse into the timid savage at the sound of his voice. Would not this well-meant but miserable trick of Jim's have the effect of increasing her unreasoning animal-like distrust of him? A few days later brought an unexpected answer to his question.

It was the hottest hour of the day. He had been fishing off the reef of rocks where he had first seen her, and had taken in his line and was leisurely pulling for the lighthouse. Suddenly a little musical cry not unlike a bird's struck his ear. He lay on his oars and listened. It was repeated; but this time it was unmistakably recognizable as the voice of the Indian girl, although he had heard it but once. He turned eagerly to the rock, but it was empty; he pulled around it, but saw nothing. He looked towards the shore, and swung his boat in that direction, when again the cry was repeated with the faintest quaver of a laugh, apparently on the level of the sea before him. For the first time he looked down, and there on the crest of a wave not a dozen yards ahead, danced the yellow hair and laughing eyes of the girl. The frightened gravity of her look was gone, lost in the flash of her white teeth and quivering dimples as her dripping face rose above the sea. When their eyes met she dived again, but quickly reappeared on the other bow, swimming with lazy, easy strokes, her smiling head thrown back over her white shoulder, as if luring him to a race. If her smile was a revelation to him, still more so was this first touch of feminine coquetry in her attitude. He pulled eagerly towards her; with a few long overhand strokes she kept her distance, or, if he approached too near, she dived like a loon, coming up astern of him with the same childlike, mocking cry. In vain he pursued her, calling her to stop in her own tongue, and laughingly protested; she easily avoided his boat at every turn. Suddenly, when they were nearly abreast of the river estuary, she rose in the water, and, waving her little hands with a gesture of farewell, turned, and curving her back like a dolphin, leaped into the surging swell of the estuary bar and was lost in its foam. It would have been madness for him to have attempted to follow in his boat, and he saw that she knew it. He waited until her yellow crest appeared in the smoother water of the river, and then rowed back. In his excitement and preoccupation he had quite forgotten his long exposure to the sun during his active exercise, and that he was poorly equipped for the cold sea-fog which the heat had brought in earlier, and which now was quietly obliterating sea and shore. This made his progress slower and more difficult, and by the time he had reached the lighthouse he was chilled to the bone.

The next morning he woke with a dull headache and great weariness, and it was with considerable difficulty that he could attend to his duties. At nightfall, feeling worse, he determined to transfer the care of the light to Jim, but was amazed to find that he had disappeared, and what was more ominous, a bottle of spirits which Pomfrey had taken from his locker the night before had disappeared too. Like all Indians, Jim's rudimentary knowledge of civilization included "fire-water;" he evidently had been tempted, had fallen, and was too ashamed or too drunk to face his master. Pomfrey, however, managed to get the light in order and working, and then, he scarcely knew how, betook himself to bed in a state of high fever. He turned from side to side racked by pain, with burning lips and pulses. Strange fancies beset him; he had noticed when he lit his light that a strange sail was looming off the estuary—a place where no sail had ever been seen or should be—and was relieved that the lighting of the tower might show the reckless or ignorant mariner his real bearings for the "Gate." At times he had heard voices above the familiar song of the surf, and tried to rise from his bed, but could not. Sometimes these voices were strange, outlandish, dissonant, in his own language, yet only partly intelligible; but through them always rang a single voice, musical, familiar, yet of a tongue not his own—hers! And then, out of his delirium—for such it proved afterwards to be—came a strange vision. He thought that he had just lit the light when, from some strange and unaccountable reason, it suddenly became dim and defied all his efforts to revive it. To add to his discomfiture, he could see quite plainly through the lantern a strange-looking vessel standing in from the sea. She was so clearly out of her course for the Gate that he knew she had not seen the light, and his limbs trembled with shame and terror as he tried in vain to rekindle the dying light. Yet to his surprise the strange ship kept steadily on, passing the dangerous reef of rocks, until she was actually in the waters of the bay. But stranger than all, swimming beneath her bows was the golden head and laughing face of the Indian girl, even as he had seen it the day before. A strange revulsion of feeling overtook him. Believing that she was luring the ship to its destruction, he ran out on the beach and strove to hail the vessel and warn it of its impending doom. But he could not speak—no sound came from his lips. And now his attention was absorbed by the ship itself. High-bowed and pooped, and curved like the crescent moon, it was the strangest craft that he had ever seen. Even as he gazed it glided on nearer and nearer, and at last beached itself noiselessly on the sands before his own feet. A score of figures as bizarre and outlandish as the ship itself now thronged its high forecastle—really a castle in shape and warlike purpose—and leaped from its ports. The common seamen were nearly naked to the waist; the officers looked more like soldiers than sailors. What struck him more strangely was that they were one and all seemingly unconscious of the existence of the lighthouse, sauntering up and down carelessly, as if on some uninhabited strand, and even talking—so far as he could understand their old bookish dialect—as if in some hitherto undiscovered land. Their ignorance of the geography of the whole coast, and even of the sea from which they came, actually aroused his critical indignation; their coarse and stupid allusions to the fair Indian swimmer as the "mermaid" that they had seen upon their bow made him more furious still. Yet he was helpless to express his contemptuous anger, or even make them conscious of his presence. Then an interval of incoherency and utter blankness followed. When he again took up the thread of his fancy the ship seemed to be lying on her beam ends on the sand; the strange arrangement of her upper deck and top-hamper, more like a dwelling than any ship he had ever seen, was fully exposed to view, while the seamen seemed to be at work with the rudest contrivances, calking and scraping her barnacled sides. He saw that phantom crew, when not working, at wassail and festivity; heard the shouts of drunken roisterers; saw the placing of a guard around some of the most uncontrollable, and later detected the stealthy escape of half a dozen sailors inland, amidst the fruitless volley fired upon them from obsolete blunderbusses. Then his strange vision transported him inland, where he saw these seamen following some Indian women. Suddenly one of them turned and ran frenziedly towards him as if seeking succor, closely pursued by one of the sailors. Pomfrey strove to reach her, struggled violently with the fearful apathy that seemed to hold his limbs, and then, as she uttered at last a little musical cry, burst his bonds and—awoke!

As consciousness slowly struggled back to him, he could see the bare wooden-like walls of his sleeping-room, the locker, the one window bright with sunlight, the open door of the tank-room, and the little staircase to the tower. There was a strange smoky and herb-like smell in the room. He made an effort to rise, but as he did so a small sunburnt hand was laid gently yet restrainingly upon his shoulder, and he heard the same musical cry as before, but this time modulated to a girlish laugh. He raised his head faintly. Half squatting, half kneeling by his bed was the yellow-haired stranger.

With the recollection of his vision still perplexing him, he said in a weak voice, "Who are you?"

Her blue eyes met his own with quick intelligence and no trace of her former timidity. A soft, caressing light had taken its place. Pointing with her finger to her breast in a childlike gesture, she said, "Me—Olooya."

"Olooya!" He remembered suddenly that Jim had always used that word in speaking of her, but until then he had always thought it was some Indian term for her distinct class.

"Olooya," he repeated. Then, with difficulty attempting to use her own tongue, he asked, "When did you come here?"

"Last night," she answered in the same tongue. "There was no witch-fire there," she continued, pointing to the tower; "when it came not, Olooya came! Olooya found white chief sick and alone. White chief could not get up! Olooya lit witch-fire for him."

"You?" he repeated in astonishment. "I lit it myself."

She looked at him pityingly, as if still recognizing his delirium, and shook her head. "White chief was sick—how can know? Olooya made witch-fire."

He cast a hurried glance at his watch hanging on the wall beside him. It had RUN DOWN, although he had wound it the last thing before going to bed. He had evidently been lying there helpless beyond the twenty-four hours!

He groaned and turned to rise, but she gently forced him down again, and gave him some herbal infusion, in which he recognized the taste of the Yerba Buena vine which grew by the river. Then she made him comprehend in her own tongue that Jim had been decoyed, while drunk, aboard a certain schooner lying off the shore at a spot where she had seen some men digging in the sands. She had not gone there, for she was afraid of the bad men, and a slight return of her former terror came into her changeful eyes. She knew how to light the witch-light; she reminded him she had been in the tower before.

"You have saved my light, and perhaps my life," he said weakly, taking her hand.

Possibly she did not understand him, for her only answer was a vague smile. But the next instant she started up, listening intently, and then with a frightened cry drew away her hand and suddenly dashed out of the building. In the midst of his amazement the door was darkened by a figure—a stranger dressed like an ordinary miner. Pausing a moment to look after the flying Olooya, the man turned and glanced around the room, and then with a coarse, familiar smile approached Pomfrey.

Bret Harte

"Hope I ain't disturbin' ye, but I allowed I'd just be neighborly and drop in—seein' as this is gov'nment property, and me and my pardners, as American citizens and tax-payers, helps to support it. We're coastin' from Trinidad down here and prospectin' along the beach for gold in the sand. Ye seem to hev a mighty soft berth of it here—nothing to do—and lots of purty half-breeds hangin' round!"

The man's effrontery was too much for Pomfrey's self-control, weakened by illness. "It IS government property," he answered hotly, "and you have no more right to intrude upon it than you have to decoy away my servant, a government employee, during my illness, and jeopardize that property."

The unexpectedness of this attack, and the sudden revelation of the fact of Pomfrey's illness in his flushed face and hollow voice apparently frightened and confused the stranger. He stammered a surly excuse, backed out of the doorway, and disappeared. An hour later Jim appeared, crestfallen, remorseful, and extravagantly penitent. Pomfrey was too weak for reproaches or inquiry, and he was thinking only of Olooya.

She did not return. His recovery in that keen air, aided, as he sometimes thought, by the herbs she had given him, was almost as rapid as his illness. The miners did not again intrude upon the lighthouse nor trouble his seclusion. When he was able to sun himself on the sands, he could see them in the distance at work on the beach. He reflected that she would not come back while they were there, and was reconciled. But one morning Jim appeared, awkward and embarrassed, leading another Indian, whom he introduced as Olooya's brother. Pomfrey's suspicions were aroused. Except that the stranger had something of the girl's superiority of manner, there was no likeness whatever to his fair-haired acquaintance. But a fury of indignation was added to his suspicions when he learned the amazing purport of their visit. It was nothing less than an offer from the alleged brother to SELL his sister to Pomfrey for forty dollars and a jug of whiskey! Unfortunately, Pomfrey's temper once more got the better of his judgment. With a scathing exposition of the laws under which the Indian and white man equally lived, and the legal punishment of kidnaping, he swept what he believed was the impostor from his presence. He was scarcely alone again before he remembered that his imprudence might affect the girl's future access to him, but it was too late now.

Still he clung to the belief that he should see her when the prospectors had departed, and he hailed with delight the breaking up of the camp near the "sweat-house" and the disappearance of the schooner. It seemed that their gold-seeking was unsuccessful; but Pomfrey was struck, on visiting the locality, to find that in their excavations in the sand at the estuary they had uncovered the decaying timbers of a ship's small boat of some ancient and obsolete construction. This made him think of his strange dream, with a vague sense of warning which he could not shake off, and on his return to the lighthouse he took from his shelves a copy of the old voyages to see how far his fancy had been affected by his reading. In the account of Drake's visit to the coast he found a footnote which he had overlooked before, and which ran as follows: "The Admiral seems to have lost several of his crew by desertion, who were supposed to have perished miserably by starvation in the inhospitable interior or by the hands of savages. But later voyagers have suggested that the deserters married Indian wives, and there is a legend that a hundred years later a singular race of half-breeds, bearing unmistakable Anglo-Saxon characteristics, was found in that locality." Pomfrey fell into a reverie of strange hypotheses and fancies. He resolved that, when he again saw Olooya, he would question her; her terror of these men might be simply racial or some hereditary transmission.

But his intention was never fulfilled. For when days and weeks had elapsed, and he had vainly haunted the river estuary and the rocky reef before the lighthouse without a sign of her, he overcame his pride sufficiently to question Jim. The man looked at him with dull astonishment.

"Olooya gone," he said.

"Gone!—where?"

The Indian made a gesture to seaward which seemed to encompass the whole Pacific.

"How? With whom?" repeated his angry yet half-frightened master.

"With white man in ship. You say YOU no want Olooya— forty dollars too much. White man give fifty dollars—takee Olooya all same."

UNDER THE EAVES

The assistant editor of the San Francisco "Daily Informer" was going home. So much of his time was spent in the office of the "Informer" that no one ever cared to know where he passed those six hours of sleep which presumably suggested a domicile. His business appointments outside the office were generally kept at the restaurant where he breakfasted and dined, or of evenings in the lobbies of theatres or the anterooms of public meetings. Yet he had a home and an interval of seclusion of which he was jealously mindful, and it was to this he was going to-night at his usual hour.

His room was in a new building on one of the larger and busier thoroughfares. The lower floor was occupied by a bank, but as it was closed before he came home, and not yet opened when he left, it did not disturb his domestic sensibilities. The same may be said of the next floor, which was devoted to stockbrokers' and companies offices, and was equally tomb-like and silent when he passed; the floor above that was a desert of empty rooms, which echoed to his footsteps night and morning, with here and there an oasis in the green sign of a mining secretary's office, with, however, the desolating announcement that it would only be "open for transfers from two to four on Saturdays." The top floor had been frankly abandoned in an unfinished state by the builder, whose ambition had "o'erleaped itself" in that sanguine era of the city's growth. There was a smell of plaster and the first coat of paint about it still, but the whole front of the building was occupied by a long room with odd "bull's-eye" windows looking out through the heavy ornamentations of the cornice over the adjacent roofs.

It had been originally intended for a club-room, but after the ill fortune which attended the letting of the floor below, and possibly because the earthquake-fearing San Franciscans had their doubts of successful hilarity at the top of so tall a building, it remained unfinished, with the two smaller rooms at its side. Its incomplete and lonely grandeur had once struck the editor during a visit of inspection, and the landlord, whom he knew, had offered to make it habitable for him at a nominal rent. It had a lavatory with a marble basin and a tap of cold water. The offer was a novel one, but he accepted it, and fitted up the apartment with some cheap second-hand furniture, quite inconsistent with the carved mantels and decorations, and made a fair sitting-room and bedroom of it. Here, on a Sunday, when its stillness was intensified, and even a passing footstep on the pavement fifty feet below was quite startling, he would sit and work by one of the quaint open windows. In the rainy season, through the filmed panes he sometimes caught a glimpse of the distant, white-capped bay, but never of the street below him.

The lights were out, but, groping his way up to the first landing, he took from a cup-boarded niche in the wall his candlestick and matches and continued the ascent to his room. The humble candlelight flickered on the ostentatious gold letters displayed on the ground-glass doors of opulent companies which he knew were famous, and rooms where millionaires met in secret conclave, but the contrast awakened only his sense of humor. Yet he was always relieved after he had reached his own floor. Possibly its incompleteness and inchoate condition made it seem less lonely than the desolation of the finished and furnished rooms below, and it was only this recollection of past human occupancy that was depressing.

He opened his door, lit the solitary gas jet that only half illuminated the long room, and, it being already past midnight, began to undress himself. This process presently brought him to that corner of his room where his bed stood, when he suddenly stopped, and his sleepy yawn changed to a gape of surprise. For, lying in the bed, its head upon the pillow, and its rigid arms accurately stretched down over the turned-back sheet, was a child's doll! It was a small doll—a banged and battered doll, that had seen service, but it had evidently been "tucked in" with maternal tenderness, and lay there with its staring eyes turned to the ceiling, the very genius of insomnia!

His first start of surprise was followed by a natural resentment of what might have been an impertinent intrusion on his privacy by some practical-joking adult, for he knew there was no child in the house.

His room was kept in order by the wife of the night watchman employed by the bank, and no one else had a right of access to it. But the woman might have brought a child there and not noticed its disposal of its plaything. He smiled. It might have been worse! It might have been a real baby!

The idea tickled him with a promise of future "copy"—of a story with farcical complications, or even a dramatic ending, in which the baby, adopted by him, should turn out to be somebody's stolen offspring. He lifted the little image that had suggested these fancies, carefully laid it on his table, went to bed, and presently forgot it all in slumber.

In the morning his good-humor and interest in it revived to

Bret Harte

the extent of writing on a slip of paper, "Good-morning! Thank you—I've slept very well," putting the slip in the doll's jointed arms, and leaving it in a sitting posture outside his door when he left his room. When he returned late at night it was gone.

But it so chanced that, a few days later, owing to press of work on the "Informer," he was obliged to forego his usual Sunday holiday out of town, and that morning found him, while the bells were ringing for church, in his room with a pile of manuscript and proof before him. For these were troublous days in San Francisco; the great Vigilance Committee of '56 was in session, and the offices of the daily papers were thronged with eager seekers of news. Such affairs, indeed, were not in the functions of the assistant editor, nor exactly to his taste; he was neither a partisan of the so-called Law and Order Party, nor yet an enthusiastic admirer of the citizen Revolutionists known as the Vigilance Committee, both extremes being incompatible with his habits of thought. Consequently he was not displeased at this opportunity of doing his work away from the office and the "heady talk" of controversy.

He worked on until the bells ceased and a more than Sabbath stillness fell upon the streets. So quiet was it that once or twice the conversation of passing pedestrians floated up and into his window, as of voices at his elbow.

Presently he heard the sound of a child's voice singing in subdued tone, as if fearful of being overheard. This time he laid aside his pen—it certainly was no delusion! The sound did not come from the open window, but from some space on a level with his room. Yet there was no contiguous building as high.

He rose and tried to open his door softly, but it creaked, and the singing instantly ceased. There was nothing before him but the bare, empty hall, with its lathed and plastered partitions, and the two smaller rooms, unfinished like his own, on either side of him. Their doors were shut; the one at his right hand was locked, the other yielded to his touch.

For the first moment he saw only the bare walls of the apparently empty room. But a second glance showed him two children—a boy of seven and a girl of five—sitting on the floor, which was further littered by a mattress, pillow, and blanket. There was a cheap tray on one of the trunks containing two soiled plates and cups and fragments of a meal. But there was neither a chair nor table nor any other article of furniture in the room. Yet he was struck by the fact that, in spite of this poverty of surrounding, the children were decently dressed, and the few scattered pieces of luggage in quality bespoke a superior condition.

The children met his astonished stare with an equal wonder and, he fancied, some little fright. The boy's lips trembled a little as he said apologetically—

"I told Jinny not to sing. But she didn't make MUCH noise."

"Mamma said I could play with my dolly. But I fordot and singed," said the little girl penitently.

"Where's your mamma?" asked the young man. The fancy of their being near relatives of the night watchman had vanished at the sound of their voices.

"Dorn out," said the girl.

"When did she go out?"

"Last night."

"Were you all alone here last night?"

"Yes!"

Perhaps they saw the look of indignation and pity in the editor's face, for the boy said quickly—

"She don't go out EVERY night; last night she went to"—

He stopped suddenly, and both children looked at each other with a half laugh and half cry, and then repeated in hopeless unison, "She's dorn out."

"When is she coming back again?"

"To-night. But we won't make any more noise."

"Who brings you your food?" continued the editor, looking at the tray.

"Woberts."

Evidently Roberts, the night watchman! The editor felt relieved; here was a clue to some explanation. He instantly sat down on the floor between them.

"So that was the dolly that slept in my bed," he said gayly, taking it up.

God gives helplessness a wonderful intuition of its friends. The children looked up at the face of their grown-up companion, giggled, and then burst into a shrill fit of laughter. He felt that it was the first one they had really indulged in for many days. Nevertheless he said, "Hush!" confidentially; why he scarcely knew, except to intimate to them that he had taken in their situation thoroughly. "Make no noise," he added softly, "and come into my big room."

They hung back, however, with frightened yet longing eyes. "Mamma said we mussent do out of this room," said the girl.

"Not ALONE," responded the editor quickly, "but with ME, you know; that's different."

The logic sufficed them, poor as it was. Their hands slid quite naturally into his. But at the door he stopped, and motioning to the locked door of the other room, asked:—

"And is that mamma's room, too?"

Their little hands slipped from his and they were silent. Presently the boy, as if acted upon by some occult influence of the girl, said in a half whisper, "Yes."

The editor did not question further, but led them into his room. Here they lost the slight restraint they had shown, and began, child fashion, to become questioners themselves.

In a few moments they were in possession of his name, his business, the kind of restaurant he frequented, where he went when he left his room all day, the meaning of those funny slips of paper, and the written manuscripts, and why he was so quiet. But any attempt of his to retaliate by counter questions was met by a sudden reserve so unchildlike and painful to him—as it was evidently to themselves—that he desisted, wisely postponing his inquiries until he could meet Roberts.

He was glad when they fell to playing games with each other quite naturally, yet not entirely forgetting his propinquity, as their occasional furtive glances at his movements showed him. He, too, became presently absorbed in his work, until it was finished and it was time for him to take it to the office of the "Informer." The wild idea seized him of also taking the children afterwards for a holiday to the Mission Dolores, but he prudently remembered that even this negligent mother of theirs might have some rights over her offspring that he was bound to respect.

He took leave of them gayly, suggesting that the doll be replaced in his bed while he was away, and even assisted in "tucking it up." But during the afternoon the recollection of these lonely playfellows in the deserted house obtruded itself upon his work and the talk of his companions. Sunday night was his busiest night, and he could not, therefore, hope to get away in time to assure himself of their mother's return.

It was nearly two in the morning when he returned to his room. He paused for a moment on the threshold to listen for any sound from the adjoining room. But all was hushed.

His intention of speaking to the night watchman was, however, anticipated the next morning by that guardian himself. A tap upon his door while he was dressing caused him to open it somewhat hurriedly in the hope of finding one of the children there, but he met only the embarrassed face of Roberts. Inviting him into the room, the editor continued dressing. Carefully closing the door behind him, the man began, with evident hesitation,—

"I oughter hev told ye suthin' afore, Mr. Breeze; but I kalkilated, so to speak, that you wouldn't be bothered one way or another, and so ye hadn't any call to know that there was folks here"—

"Oh, I see," interrupted Breeze cheerfully; "you're speaking of the family next door—the landlord's new tenants."

"They ain't exactly THAT," said Roberts, still with embarrassment. "The fact is—ye see—the thing points THIS way: they ain't no right to be here, and it's as much as my place is worth if it leaks out that they are."

Mr. Breeze suspended his collar-buttoning, and stared at Roberts.

"You see, sir, they're mighty poor, and they've nowhere else to go—and I reckoned to take 'em in here for a spell and say nothing about it."

"But the landlord wouldn't object, surely? I'll speak to him myself," said Breeze impulsively.

"Oh, no; don't!" said Roberts in alarm; "he wouldn't like it. You see, Mr. Breeze, it's just this way: the mother, she's a born lady, and did my old woman a good turn in old times when the family was rich; but now she's obliged—just to support herself, you know—to take up with what she gets, and she acts in the bally in the theatre, you see, and hez to come in late o' nights. In them cheap boarding-houses, you know, the folks looks down upon her for that, and won't hev her, and in the cheap hotels the men are—you know—a darned sight wuss, and that's how I took her and her kids in here, where no one knows 'em."

"I see," nodded the editor sympathetically; "and very good it was of you, my man."

Roberts looked still more confused, and stammered with a forced laugh, "And—so—I'm just keeping her on here, unbeknownst, until her husband gets"—He stopped suddenly.

"So she has a husband living, then?" said Breeze in surprise.

"In the mines, yes—in the mines!" repeated Roberts with a monotonous deliberation quite distinct from his previous hesitation, "and she's only waitin' until he gets money enough—to—to take her away." He stopped and breathed hard.

"But couldn't you—couldn't WE—get her some more furniture? There's nothing in that room, you know, not a chair or table; and unless the other room is better furnished"—

"Eh? Oh, yes!" said Roberts quickly, yet still with a certain embarrassment; "of course THAT'S better furnished, and she's quite satisfied, and so are the kids, with anything. And now, Mr. Breeze, I reckon you'll say nothin' o' this, and you'll never go back on me?"

"My dear Mr. Roberts," said the editor gravely, "from this moment I am not only blind, but deaf to the fact that ANYBODY occupies this floor but myself."

"I knew you was white all through, Mr. Breeze," said the night watchman, grasping the young man's hand with a grip of iron, "and I telled my wife so. I sez, 'Jest you let me tell him EVERYTHIN',' but she"—He stopped again and became confused.

"And she was quite right, I dare say," said Breeze, with a laugh; "and I do not want to know anything. And that poor woman must never know that I ever knew anything, either. But you may tell your wife that when the mother is away she can bring the little ones in here whenever she likes."

"Thank ye—thank ye, sir!—and I'll just run down and tell the old woman now, and won't intrude upon your dressin' any longer."

He grasped Breeze's hand again, went out and closed the door behind him. It might have been the editor's fancy, but he thought there was a certain interval of silence outside the door before the night watchman's heavy tread was heard along the hall again.

For several evenings after this Mr. Breeze paid some attention to the ballet in his usual round of the theatres. Although he had never seen his fair neighbor, he had a vague idea that he might recognize her through some likeness to her children. But in vain. In the opulent charms of certain nymphs, and in the angular austerities of others, he failed equally to discern any of those refinements which might have distinguished the "born lady" of Roberts's story, or which he himself had seen in her children.

These he did not meet again during the week, as his duties kept him late at the office; but from certain signs in his room he knew that Mrs. Roberts had availed herself of his invitation to bring them in with her, and he regularly found "Jinny's" doll tucked up in his bed at night, and he as regularly disposed of it outside his door in the morning, with a few sweets, like an offering, tucked under its rigid arms.

But another circumstance touched him more delicately; his room was arranged with greater care than before, and with an occasional exhibition of taste that certainly had not distinguished Mrs. Roberts's previous ministrations. One evening on his return he found a small bouquet of inexpensive flowers in a glass on his writing-table. He loved flowers too well not to detect that they were quite fresh, and could have been put there only an hour or two before he arrived.

The next evening was Saturday, and, as he usually left the office earlier on that day, it occurred to him, as he walked home, that it was about the time his fair neighbor would be leaving the theatre, and that it was possible he might meet her.

At the front door, however, he found Roberts, who returned his greeting with a certain awkwardness which struck him as singular. When he reached the niche on the landing he found his candle was gone, but he proceeded on, groping his way up the stairs, with an odd conviction that both these incidents pointed to the fact that the woman had just returned or was expected.

He had also a strange feeling—which may have been owing to the darkness—that some one was hidden on the landing or on the stairs where he would pass. This was further accented by a faint odor of patchouli, as, with his hand on the rail, he turned the corner of the third landing, and he was convinced that if he had put out his other hand it would have come in contact with his mysterious neighbor. But a certain instinct of respect for her secret, which she was even now guarding in the darkness, withheld him, and he passed on quickly to his own floor.

Here it was lighter; the moon shot a beam of silver across the passage from an unshuttered window as he passed. He reached his room door, entered, but instead of lighting the gas and shutting the door, stood with it half open, listening in the darkness.

His suspicions were verified; there was a slight rustling noise, and a figure which had evidently followed him appeared at the end of the passage. It was that of a woman habited in a grayish dress and cloak of the same color; but as she passed across the band of moonlight he had a distinct view of her anxious, worried face. It was a face no longer young; it was worn with illness, but still replete with a delicacy and faded beauty so inconsistent with her avowed profession that he felt a sudden pang of pain and doubt. The next moment she had vanished in her room, leaving the same faint perfume behind her. He closed his door softly, lit the gas, and sat down in a state of perplexity. That swift glimpse of her face and figure had made her story improbable to the point of absurdity, or possibly to the extreme of pathos!

It seemed incredible that a woman of that quality should be forced to accept a vocation at once so low, so distasteful, and so unremunerative. With her evident antecedents, had she no friends but this common Western night watchman of a bank? Had Roberts deceived him? Was his whole story a fabrication, and was there some complicity between the two? What was it? He knit his brows.

Mr. Breeze had that overpowering knowledge of the world which only comes with the experience of twenty-five, and to this he superadded the active imagination of a newspaper man. A plot to rob the bank? These mysterious absences, that luggage which he doubted not was empty and intended for spoil! But why encumber herself with the two children? Here his common sense and instinct of the ludicrous returned and he smiled.

But he could not believe in the ballet dancer! He wondered, indeed, how any manager could have accepted the grim satire of that pale, worried face among the fairies, that sad refinement amid their vacant smiles and rouged checks. And then, growing sad again, he comforted himself with the reflection that at least the children were not alone that night, and so went to sleep.

For some days he had no further meeting with his neighbors. The disturbed state of the city—for the Vigilance Committee were still in session—obliged the daily press to issue "extras," and his work at the office increased.

It was not until Sunday again that he was able to be at home. Needless to say that his solitary little companions were duly installed there, while he sat at work with his proofs on the table before him.

The stillness of the empty house was only broken by the habitually subdued voices of the children at their play, when suddenly the harsh stroke of a distant bell came through the open window. But it was no Sabbath bell, and Mr. Breeze knew it. It was the tocsin of the Vigilance Committee, summoning the members to assemble at their quarters for a capture, a trial, or an execution of some wrongdoer. To him it was equally a summons to the office—to distasteful news and excitement.

He threw his proofs aside in disgust, laid down his pen, seized his hat, and paused a moment to look round for his playmates. But they were gone! He went into the hall, looked into the open door of their room, but they were not there. He tried the door of the second room, but it was locked.

Satisfied that they had stolen downstairs in their eagerness to know what the bell meant, he hurried down also, met Roberts in the passage,—a singularly unusual circumstance at that hour,—called to him to look after the runaways, and hurried to his office.

Here he found the staff collected, excitedly discussing the news. One of the Vigilance Committee prisoners, a notorious bully and ruffian, detained as a criminal and a witness, had committed suicide in his cell. Fortunately this was all reportorial work, and the services of Mr. Breeze were not required. He hurried back, relieved, to his room.

When he reached his landing, breathlessly, he heard the same quick rustle he had heard that memorable evening, and was quite satisfied that he saw a figure glide swiftly out of the open door of his room. It was no doubt his neighbor, who had been seeking her children, and as he heard their voices as he passed, his uneasiness and suspicions were removed.

He sat down again to his scattered papers and proofs, finished his work, and took it to the office on his way to dinner. He returned early, in the hope that he might meet his neighbor again, and had quite settled his mind that he was justified in offering a civil "Good-evening" to her, in spite of his previous respectful ignoring of her presence. She must certainly have become aware by this time of his attention to her children and consideration for herself, and could not mistake his motives. But he was disappointed, although he came up softly; he found the floor in darkness and silence on his return, and he had to be content with lighting his gas and settling down to work again.

A near church clock had struck ten when he was startled by the sound of an unfamiliar and uncertain step in the hall, followed by a tap at his door. Breeze jumped to his feet, and was astonished to find Dick, the "printer's devil," standing on the threshold with a roll of proofs in his hand.

"How did you get here?" he asked testily.

"They told me at the restaurant they reckoned you lived yere, and the night watchman at the door headed me straight up. When he knew whar I kem from he wanted to know what the news was, but I told him he'd better buy an extra and see."

"Well, what did you come for?" said the editor impatiently.

"The foreman said it was important, and he wanted to know

afore he went to press ef this yer correction was YOURS?"

He went to the table, unrolled the proofs, and, taking out the slip, pointed to a marked paragraph. "The foreman says the reporter who brought the news allows he got it straight first-hand! But ef you've corrected it, he reckons you know best."

Breeze saw at a glance that the paragraph alluded to was not of his own writing, but one of several news items furnished by reporters. These had been "set up" in the same "galley," and consequently appeared in the same proof-slip. He was about to say curtly that neither the matter nor the correction was his, when something odd in the correction of the item struck him. It read as follows:—

"It appears that the notorious 'Jim Bodine,' who is in hiding and badly wanted by the Vigilance Committee, has been tempted lately into a renewal of his old recklessness. He was seen in Sacramento Street the other night by two separate witnesses, one of whom followed him, but he escaped in some friendly doorway."

The words "in Sacramento Street" were stricken out and replaced by the correction "on the Saucelito shore," and the words "friendly doorway" were changed to "friendly dinghy." The correction was not his, nor the handwriting, which was further disguised by being an imitation of print. A strange idea seized him.

"Has any one seen these proofs since I left them at the office?"

"No, only the foreman, sir."

He remembered that he had left the proofs lying openly on his table when he was called to the office at the stroke of the alarm bell; he remembered the figure he saw gliding from his room on his return. She had been there alone with the proofs; she only could have tampered with them.

The evident object of the correction was to direct the public attention from Sacramento Street to Saucelito, as the probable whereabouts of this "Jimmy Bodine." The street below was Sacramento Street, the "friendly doorway" might have been their own.

That she had some knowledge of this Bodine was not more improbable than the ballet story. Her strange absences, the mystery surrounding her, all seemed to testify that she had some connection—perhaps only an innocent one—with these desperate people whom the Vigilance Committee were hunting down. Her attempt to save the man was, after all, no more illegal than their attempt to capture him. True, she might have trusted him, Breeze, without this tampering with his papers; yet perhaps she thought he was certain to discover it—and it was only a silent appeal to his mercy. The corrections were ingenious and natural—it was the act of an intelligent, quick-witted woman.

Mr. Breeze was prompt in acting upon his intuition, whether right or wrong. He took up his pen, wrote on the margin of the proof, "Print as corrected," said to the boy carelessly, "The corrections are all right," and dismissed him quickly.

The corrected paragraph which appeared in the "Informer" the next morning seemed to attract little public attention, the greater excitement being the suicide of the imprisoned bully and the effect it might have upon the prosecution of other suspected parties, against whom the dead man had been expected to bear witness.

Mr. Breeze was unable to obtain any information regarding

the desperado Bodine's associates and relations; his correction of the paragraph had made the other members of the staff believe he had secret and superior information regarding the fugitive, and he thus was estopped from asking questions. But he felt himself justified now in demanding fuller information from Roberts at the earliest opportunity.

For this purpose he came home earlier that night, hoping to find the night watchman still on his first beat in the lower halls. But he was disappointed. He was amazed, however, on reaching his own landing, to find the passage piled with new luggage, some of that ruder type of rolled blanket and knapsack known as a "miner's kit." He was still more surprised to hear men's voices and the sound of laughter proceeding from the room that was always locked. A sudden sense of uneasiness and disgust, he knew not why, came over him.

He passed quickly into his room, shut the door sharply, and lit the gas. But he presently heard the door of the locked room open, a man's voice, slightly elevated by liquor and opposition, saying, "I know what's due from one gen'leman to 'nother"—a querulous, objecting voice saying, "Hole on! not now," and a fainter feminine protest, all of which were followed by a rap on his door.

Breeze opened it to two strangers, one of whom lurched forward unsteadily with outstretched hand. He had a handsome face and figure, and a certain consciousness of it even in the abandon of liquor; he had an aggressive treacherousness of eye which his potations had not subdued. He grasped Breeze's hand tightly, but dropped it the next moment perfunctorily as he glanced round the room.

"I told them I was bound to come in," he said, without looking at Breeze, "and say 'Howdy!' to the man that's bin a pal to my women folks and the kids—and acted white all through! I said to Mame, 'I reckon HE knows who I am, and that I kin be high-toned to them that's high-toned; kin return shake for shake and shot for shot!' Aye! that's me! So I was bound to come in like a gen'leman, sir, and here I am!"

He threw himself in an unproffered chair and stared at Breeze.

"I'm afraid," said Breeze dryly, "that, nevertheless, I never knew who you were, and that even now I am ignorant whom I am addressing."

"That's just it," said the second man, with a querulous protest, which did not, however, conceal his admiring vassalage to his friend; "that's what I'm allus telling Jim. 'Jim,' I says, 'how is folks to know you're the man that shot Kernel Baxter, and dropped three o' them Mariposa Vigilants? They didn't see you do it! They just look at your fancy style and them mustaches of yours, and allow ye might be death on the girls, but they don't know ye! An' this man yere—he's a scribe in them papers—writes what the boss editor tells him, and lives up yere on the roof, 'longside yer wife and the children—what's he knowin' about YOU?' Jim's all right enough," he continued, in easy confidence to Breeze, "but he's too fresh 'bout himself."

Mr. James Bodine accepted this tribute and criticism of his henchman with a complacent laugh, which was not, however, without a certain contempt for the speaker and the man spoken to. His bold, selfish eyes wandered round the room as if in search of some other amusement than his companions offered.

"I reckon this is the room which that hound of a landlord, Rakes, allowed he'd fix up for our poker club—the club that

Dan Simmons and me got up, with a few other sports. It was to be a slap-up affair, right under the roof, where there was no chance of the police raiding us. But the cur weakened when the Vigilants started out to make war on any game a gen'leman might hev that wasn't in their gummy-bag, salt pork trade. Well, it's gettin' a long time between drinks, gen'lemen, ain't it?" He looked round him significantly.

Only the thought of the woman and her children in the next room, and the shame that he believed she was enduring, enabled Breeze to keep his temper or even a show of civility.

"I'm afraid," he said quietly, "that you'll find very little here to remind you of the club—not even the whiskey; for I use the room only as a bedroom, and as I am a workingman, and come in late and go out early, I have never found it available for hospitality, even to my intimate friends. I am very glad, however, that the little leisure I have had in it has enabled me to make the floor less lonely for your children."

Mr. Bodine got up with an affected yawn, turned an embarrassed yet darkening eye on Breeze, and lunged unsteadily to the door. "And as I only happened in to do the reg'lar thing between high-toned gen'lemen, I reckon we kin say 'Quits.'" He gave a coarse laugh, said "So long," nodded, stumbled into the passage, and thence into the other room.

His companion watched him pass out with a relieved yet protecting air, and then, closing the door softly, drew nearer to Breeze, and said in husky confidence,—

"Ye ain't seein' him at his best, mister! He's bin drinkin' too much, and this yer news has upset him."

"What news?" asked Breeze.

"This yer suicide o' Irish Jack!"

"Was he his friend?"

"Friend?" ejaculated the man, horrified at the mere suggestion. "Not much! Why, Irish Jack was the only man that could hev hung Jim! Now he's dead, in course the Vigilants ain't got no proof agin Jim. Jim wants to face it out now an' stay here, but his wife and me don't see it noways! So we are taking advantage o' the lull agin him to get him off down the coast this very night. That's why he's been off his head drinkin'. Ye see, when a man has been for weeks hidin'—part o' the time in that room and part o' the time on the wharf, where them Vigilants has been watchin' every ship that left in order to ketch him, he's inclined to celebrate his chance o' getting away"—

"Part of the time in that room?" interrupted Breeze quickly.

"Sartin! Don't ye see? He allus kem in as you went out—sabe!—and got away before you kem back, his wife all the time just a-hoverin' between the two places, and keeping watch for him. It was killin' to her, you see, for she wasn't brought up to it, whiles Jim didn't keer—had two revolvers and kalkilated to kill a dozen Vigilants afore he dropped. But that's over now, and when I've got him safe on that 'plunger' down at the wharf to-night, and put him aboard the schooner that's lying off the Heads, he's all right again."

"And Roberts knew all this and was one of his friends?" asked Breeze.

"Roberts knew it, and Roberts's wife used to be a kind of servant to Jim's wife in the South, when she was a girl, but I don't know ez Roberts is his FRIEND!"

"He certainly has shown himself one," said Breeze.

"Ye-e-s," said the stranger meditatively, "ye-e-s." He stopped, opened the door softly, and peeped out, and then closed it again softly. "It's sing'lar, Mr. Breeze," he went on in a sudden yet embarrassed burst of confidence, "that Jim thar—a man thet can shoot straight, and hez frequent; a man thet knows every skin game goin'—that THET man Jim," very slowly, "hezn't really—got—any friends—'cept me—and his wife."

"Indeed?" said Mr. Breeze dryly.

"Sure! Why, you yourself didn't cotton to him—I could see THET."

Mr. Breeze felt himself redden slightly, and looked curiously at the man. This vulgar parasite, whom he had set down as a worshiper of sham heroes, undoubtedly did not look like an associate of Bodine's, and had a certain seriousness that demanded respect. As he looked closer into his wide, round face, seamed with small-pox, he fancied he saw even in its fatuous imbecility something of that haunting devotion he had seen on the refined features of the wife. He said more gently,—

"But one friend like you would seem to be enough."

"I ain't what I uster be, Mr. Breeze," said the man meditatively, "and mebbe ye don't know who I am. I'm Abe Shuckster, of Shuckster's Ranch—one of the biggest in Petalumy. I was a rich man until a year ago, when Jim got inter trouble. What with mortgages and interest, payin' up Jim's friends and buying off some ez was set agin him, thar ain't much left, and when I've settled that bill for the schooner lying off the Heads there I reckon I'm about played out. But I've allus a shanty at Petalumy, and mebbe when things is froze over and Jim gets back—you'll come and see him—for you ain't seen him at his best."

"I suppose his wife and children go with him?" said Breeze.

"No! He's agin it, and wants them to come later. But that's all right, for you see she kin go back to their own house at the Mission, now that the Vigilants are givin' up shadderin' it. So long, Mr. Breeze! We're startin' afore daylight. Sorry you didn't see Jim in condition."

He grasped Breeze's hand warmly and slipped out of the door softly. For an instant Mr. Breeze felt inclined to follow him into the room and make a kinder adieu to the pair, but the reflection that he might embarrass the wife, who, it would seem, had purposely avoided accompanying her husband when he entered, withheld him. And for the last few minutes he had been doubtful if he had any right to pose as her friend. Beside the devotion of the man who had just left him, his own scant kindness to her children seemed ridiculous.

He went to bed, but tossed uneasily until he fancied he heard stealthy footsteps outside his door and in the passage. Even then he thought of getting up, dressing, and going out to bid farewell to the fugitives. But even while he was thinking of it he fell asleep and did not wake until the sun was shining in at his windows.

He sprang to his feet, threw on his dressing-gown, and peered into the passage. Everything was silent. He stepped outside—the light streamed into the hall from the open doors and windows of both rooms—the floor was empty; not a trace of the former occupants remained. He was turning back when his eye fell upon the battered wooden doll set upright

Bret Harte

against his doorjamb, holding stiffly in its jointed arms a bit of paper folded like a note. Opening it, he found a few lines written in pencil.

God bless you for your kindness to us, and try to forgive me for touching your papers. But I thought that you would detect it, know WHY I did it, and then help us, as you did! Good-by!

MAMIE BODINE.

Mr. Breeze laid down the paper with a slight accession of color, as if its purport had been ironical. How little had he done compared to the devotion of this delicate woman or the sacrifices of that rough friend! How deserted looked this nest under the eaves, which had so long borne its burden of guilt, innocence, shame, and suffering! For many days afterwards he avoided it except at night, and even then he often found himself lying awake to listen to the lost voices of the children.

But one evening, a fortnight later, he came upon Roberts in the hall. "Well," said Breeze, with abrupt directness, "did he get away?"

Roberts started, uttered an oath which it is possible the Recording Angel passed to his credit, and said, "Yes, HE got away all right!"

"Why, hasn't his wife joined him?"

"No. Never, in this world, I reckon; and if anywhere in the next, I don't want to go there!" said Roberts furiously.

"Is he dead?"

"Dead? That kind don't die!"

"What do you mean?"

Roberts's lips writhed, and then, with a strong effort, he said with deliberate distinctness, "I mean—that the hound went off with another woman—that—was—in—that schooner, and left that fool Shuckster adrift in the plunger."

"And the wife and children?"

"Shuckster sold his shanty at Petaluma to pay their passage to the States. Good-night!"

HOW REUBEN ALLEN "SAW LIFE" IN SAN FRANCISCO

The junior partner of the firm of Sparlow & Kane, "Druggists and Apothecaries," of San Francisco, was gazing meditatively out of the corner of the window of their little shop in Dupont Street. He could see the dimly lit perspective of the narrow thoroughfare fade off into the level sand wastes of Market Street on the one side, and plunge into the half-excavated bulk of Telegraph Hill on the other. He could see the glow and hear the rumble of Montgomery Street—the great central avenue farther down the hill. Above the housetops was spread the warm blanket of sea-fog under which the city was regularly laid to sleep every summer night to the cool lullaby of the Northwest Trades. It was already half-past eleven; footsteps on the wooden pavement were getting rarer and more remote; the last cart had rumbled by; the shutters were up along the street; the glare of his own red and blue jars was the only beacon left to guide the wayfarers. Ordinarily he would have been going home at this hour, when his partner, who occupied the surgery and a small bedroom at the rear of the shop, always returned to relieve him. That night, however, a professional visit would detain the "Doctor" until half-past twelve. There was still an hour to wait. He felt drowsy; the mysterious incense of the shop, that combined essence of drugs, spice, scented soap, and orris root—which always reminded him of the Arabian

Nights—was affecting him. He yawned, and then, turning away, passed behind the counter, took down a jar labeled "Glycyrr. Glabra," selected a piece of Spanish licorice, and meditatively sucked it. Not receiving from it that diversion and sustenance he apparently was seeking, he also visited, in an equally familiar manner, a jar marked "Jujubes," and returned ruminatingly to his previous position.

If I have not in this incident sufficiently established the youthfulness of the junior partner, I may add briefly that he was just nineteen, that he had early joined the emigration to California, and after one or two previous light-hearted essays at other occupations, for which he was singularly unfitted, he had saved enough to embark on his present venture, still less suited to his temperament. In those adventurous days trades and vocations were not always filled by trained workmen; it was extremely probable that the experienced chemist was already making his success as a gold-miner, with a lawyer and a physician for his partners, and Mr. Kane's inexperienced position was by no means a novel one. A slight knowledge of Latin as a written language, an American schoolboy's acquaintance with chemistry and natural philosophy, were deemed sufficient by his partner, a regular physician, for practical cooperation in the vending of drugs and putting up of prescriptions. He knew the difference between acids and alkalies and the peculiar results which attended their incautious combination. But he was excessively deliberate, painstaking, and cautious. The legend which adorned the desk at the counter, "Physicians' prescriptions carefully prepared," was more than usually true as regarded the adverb. There was no danger of his poisoning anybody through haste or carelessness, but it was possible that an urgent "case" might have succumbed to the disease while he was putting up the remedy. Nor was his caution entirely passive. In those days the "heroic" practice of medicine was in keeping with the abnormal development of the country; there were "record" doses of calomel and quinine, and he had once or twice incurred the fury of local practitioners by sending back their prescriptions with a modest query.

The far-off clatter of carriage wheels presently arrested his attention; looking down the street, he could see the lights of a hackney carriage advancing towards him. They had already flashed upon the open crossing a block beyond before his vague curiosity changed into an active instinctive presentiment that they were coming to the shop. He withdrew to a more becoming and dignified position behind the counter as the carriage drew up with a jerk before the door.

The driver rolled from his box and opened the carriage door to a woman whom he assisted, between some hysterical exclamations on her part and some equally incoherent explanations of his own, into the shop. Kane saw at a glance that both were under the influence of liquor, and one, the woman, was disheveled and bleeding about the head. Yet she was elegantly dressed and evidently en fete, with one or two "tricolor" knots and ribbons mingled with her finery. Her golden hair, matted and darkened with blood, had partly escaped from her French bonnet and hung heavily over her shoulders. The driver, who was supporting her roughly, and with a familiarity that was part of the incongruous spectacle, was the first to speak.

"Madame le Blank! ye know! Got cut about the head down at the fete at South Park! Tried to dance upon the table, and rolled over on some champagne bottles. See? Wants plastering up!"

"Ah brute! Hog! Nozzing of ze kine! Why will you lie? I dance! Ze cowards, fools, traitors zere upset ze table and I fall. I am cut! Ah, my God, how I am cut!"

She stopped suddenly and lapsed heavily against the counter. At which Kane hurried around to support her into the surgery with the one fixed idea in his bewildered mind of getting her out of the shop, and, suggestively, into the domain and under the responsibility of his partner. The hackman, apparently relieved and washing his hands of any further complicity in the matter, nodded and smiled, and saying, "I reckon I'll wait outside, pardner," retreated incontinently to his vehicle. To add to Kane's half-ludicrous embarrassment the fair patient herself slightly resisted his support, accused the hackman of "abandoning her," and demanded if Kane knew "zee reason of zees affair," yet she presently lapsed again into the large reclining-chair which he had wheeled forward, with open mouth, half-shut eyes, and a strange Pierrette mask of face, combined of the pallor of faintness and chalk, and the rouge of paint and blood. At which Kane's cautiousness again embarrassed him. A little brandy from the bottle labeled "Vini Galli" seemed to be indicated, but his inexperience could not determine if her relaxation was from bloodlessness or the reacting depression of alcohol. In this dilemma he chose a medium course, with aromatic spirits of ammonia, and mixing a diluted quantity in a measuring-glass, poured it between her white lips. A start, a struggle, a cough—a volley of imprecatory French, and the knocking of the glass from his hand followed—but she came to! He quickly sponged her head of the half-coagulated blood, and removed a few fragments of glass from a long laceration of the scalp. The shock of the cold water and the appearance of the ensanguined basin frightened her into a momentary passivity. But when Kane found it necessary to cut her hair in the region of the wound in order to apply the adhesive plaster, she again endeavored to rise and grasp the scissors.

"You'll bleed to death if you're not quiet," said the young man with dogged gravity.

Something in his manner impressed her into silence again. He cut whole locks away ruthlessly; he was determined to draw the edges of the wound together with the strip of plaster and stop the bleeding—if he cropped the whole head. His excessive caution for her physical condition did not extend to her superficial adornment. Her yellow tresses lay on the floor, her neck and shoulders were saturated with water from the sponge which he continually applied, until the heated strips of plaster had closed the wound almost hermetically. She whimpered, tears ran down her cheeks; but so long as it was not blood the young man was satisfied.

In the midst of it he heard the shop door open, and presently the sound of rapping on the counter. Another customer!

Mr. Kane called out, "Wait a moment," and continued his ministrations. After a pause the rapping recommenced. Kane was just securing the last strip of plaster and preserved a preoccupied silence. Then the door flew open abruptly and a figure appeared impatiently on the threshold. It was that of a miner recently returned from the gold diggings—so recently that he evidently had not had time to change his clothes at his adjacent hotel, and stood there in his high boots, duck trousers, and flannel shirt, over which his coat was slung like a hussar's jacket from his shoulder. Kane would have uttered an indignant protest at the intrusion, had not the intruder himself as quickly recoiled with an astonishment and contrition that was beyond the effect of any reproval. He literally gasped at the spectacle before him. A handsomely dressed woman reclining in a chair; lace and jewelry and ribbons depending from her saturated shoulders; tresses of golden hair filling her lap and lying on the floor; a pail of ruddy water and a sponge at her feet, and a pale young man bending over her head with a spirit lamp and strips of yellow plaster!

"'Scuse me, pard! I was just dropping in; don't you hurry! I kin wait," he stammered, falling back, and then the door closed abruptly behind him.

Kane gathered up the shorn locks, wiped the face and neck of his patient with a clean towel and his own handkerchief, threw her gorgeous opera cloak over her shoulders, and assisted her to rise. She did so, weakly but obediently; she was evidently stunned and cowed in some mysterious way by his material attitude, perhaps, or her sudden realization of her position; at least the contrast between her aggressive entrance into the shop and her subdued preparation for her departure was so remarkable that it affected even Kane's preoccupation.

"There," he said, slightly relaxing his severe demeanor with an encouraging smile, "I think this will do; we've stopped the bleeding. It will probably smart a little as the plaster sets closer. I can send my partner, Dr. Sparlow, to you in the morning."

She looked at him curiously and with a strange smile. "And zees Doctor Sparrlow—eez he like you, M'sieu?"

"He is older, and very well known," said the young man seriously. "I can safely recommend him."

"Ah," she repeated, with a pensive smile which made Kane think her quite pretty. "Ah—he ez older—your Doctor Sparrlow—but YOU are strong, M'sieu."

"And," said Kane vaguely, "he will tell you what to do."

"Ah," she repeated again softly, with the same smile, "he will tell me what to do if I shall not know myself. Dat ez good."

Kane had already wrapped her shorn locks in a piece of spotless white paper and tied it up with narrow white ribbon in the dainty fashion dear to druggists' clerks. As he handed it to her she felt in her pocket and produced a handful of gold.

"What shall I pay for zees, M'sieu?"

Kane reddened a little—solely because of his slow arithmetical faculties. Adhesive plaster was cheap—he would like to have charged proportionately for the exact amount he had used; but the division was beyond him! And he lacked the trader's instinct.

"Twenty-five cents, I think," he hazarded briefly.

She started, but smiled again. "Twenty-five cents for all zees—ze medicine, ze strips for ze head, ze hair cut"—she glanced at the paper parcel he had given her—"it is only twenty-five cents?"

"That's all."

He selected from her outstretched palm, with some difficulty, the exact amount, the smallest coin it held. She again looked at him curiously—half confusedly—and moved slowly into the shop. The miner, who was still there, retreated as before with a gaspingly apologetic gesture—even flattening himself against the window to give her sweeping silk flounces freer passage. As she passed into the street with a "Merci, M'sieu, good a'night," and the hackman started from the vehicle to receive her, the miner drew a long breath, and bringing his fist down upon the counter, ejaculated,—

"B'gosh! She's a stunner!"

Kane, a good deal relieved at her departure and the success of his ministration, smiled benignly.

The stranger again stared after the retreating carriage, looked around the shop, and even into the deserted surgery, and approached the counter confidentially. "Look yer, pardner. I kem straight from St. Jo, Mizzorri, to Gold Hill—whar I've got a claim—and I reckon this is the first time I ever struck San Francisker. I ain't up to towny ways nohow, and I allow that mebbe I'm rather green. So we'll let that pass! Now look yer!" he added, leaning over the counter with still deeper and even mysterious confidence, "I suppose this yer kind o' thing is the regular go here, eh? nothin' new to YOU! in course no! But to me, pard, it's just fetchin' me! Lifts me clear outer my boots every time! Why, when I popped into that thar room, and saw that lady—all gold, furbelows, and spangles—at twelve o'clock at night, sittin' in that cheer and you a-cuttin' her h'r and swabbin' her head o' blood, and kinder prospectin' for 'indications,' so to speak, and doin' it so kam and indifferent like, I sez to myself, 'Rube, Rube,' sez I, 'this yer's life! city life! San Francisker life! and b'gosh, you've dropped into it! Now, pard, look yar! don't you answer, ye know, ef it ain't square and above board for me to know; I ain't askin' you to give the show away, ye know, in the matter of high-toned ladies like that, but" (very mysteriously, and sinking his voice to the lowest confidential pitch, as he put his hand to his ear as if to catch the hushed reply), "what mout hev bin happening, pard?"

Considerably amused at the man's simplicity, Kane replied good-humoredly: "Danced among some champagne bottles on a table at a party, fell and got cut by glass."

The stranger nodded his head slowly and approvingly as he repeated with infinite deliberateness: "Danced on champagne bottles, champagne! you said, pard? at a pahty! Yes!"

(musingly and approvingly). "I reckon that's about the gait they take. SHE'D do it."

"Is there anything I can do for you? sorry to have kept you waiting," said Kane, glancing at the clock.

"O ME! Lord! ye needn't mind me. Why, I should wait for anythin' o' the like o' that, and be just proud to do it! And ye see, I sorter helped myself while you war busy."

"Helped yourself?" said Kane in astonishment.

"Yes, outer that bottle." He pointed to the ammonia bottle, which still stood on the counter. "It seemed to be handy and popular."

"Man! you might have poisoned yourself."

The stranger paused a moment at the idea. "So I mout, I reckon," he said musingly, "that's so! pizined myself jest ez you was lookin' arter that high-toned case, and kinder bothered you! It's like me!"

"I mean it required diluting; you ought to have taken it in water," said Kane.

"I reckon! It DID sorter h'ist me over to the door for a little fresh air at first! seemed rayther scaldy to the lips. But wot of it that GOT THAR," he put his hand gravely to his stomach, "did me pow'ful good."

"What was the matter with you?" asked Kane.

"Well, ye see, pard" (confidentially again), "I reckon it's suthin' along o' my heart. Times it gets to poundin' away like a quartz stamp, and then it stops suddent like, and kinder leaves ME out too."

Kane looked at him more attentively. He was a strong, powerfully built man with a complexion that betrayed nothing more serious than the effects of mining cookery. It was evidently a common case of indigestion.

"I don't say it would not have done you some good if properly administered," he replied. "If you like I'll put up a diluted quantity and directions?"

"That's me, every time, pardner!" said the stranger with an accent of relief. "And look yer, don't you stop at that! Ye just put me up some samples like of anythin' you think mout be likely to hit. I'll go in for a fair show, and then meander in every now and then, betwixt times, to let you know. Ye don't mind my drifting in here, do ye? It's about ez likely a place ez I struck since I've left the Sacramento boat, and my hotel, just round the corner. Ye just sample me a bit o' everythin'; don't mind the expense. I'll take YOUR word for it. The way you—a young fellow—jest stuck to your work in thar, cool and kam as a woodpecker—not minding how high-toned she was—nor the jewelery and spangles she had on—jest got me! I sez to myself, 'Rube,' sez I, 'whatever's wrong o' YOUR insides, you jest stick to that feller to set ye right.'"

The junior partner's face reddened as he turned to his shelves ostensibly for consultation. Conscious of his inexperience, the homely praise of even this ignorant man was not ungrateful. He felt, too, that his treatment of the Frenchwoman, though successful, might not be considered remunerative from a business point of view by his partner. He accordingly acted upon the suggestion of the stranger and put up two or three specifics for dyspepsia. They were received with grateful alacrity and the casual display of considerable gold in the stranger's pocket in the process of payment. He was evidently a successful miner.

After bestowing the bottles carefully about his person, he again leaned confidentially towards Kane. "I reckon of course you know this high-toned lady, being in the way of seein' that kind o' folks. I suppose you won't mind telling me, ez a stranger. But" (he added hastily, with a deprecatory wave of his hand), "perhaps ye would."

Mr. Kane, in fact, had hesitated. He knew vaguely and by report that Madame le Blanc was the proprietress of a famous restaurant, over which she had rooms where private gambling was carried on to a great extent. It was also alleged that she was protected by a famous gambler and a somewhat notorious bully. Mr. Kane's caution suggested that he had no right to expose the reputation of his chance customer. He was silent.

The stranger's face became intensely sympathetic and apologetic. "I see!—not another word, pard! It ain't the square thing to be givin' her away, and I oughtn't to hev asked. Well—so long! I reckon I'll jest drift back to the hotel. I ain't been in San Francisker mor' 'n three hours, and I calkilate, pard, that I've jest seen about ez square a sample of high-toned life as fellers ez haz bin here a year. Well, hastermanyanner—ez the Greasers say. I'll be droppin' in to-morrow. My name's Reuben Allen o' Mariposa. I know yours; it's on the sign, and it ain't Sparlow."

He cast another lingering glance around the shop, as if loath to leave it, and then slowly sauntered out of the door, pausing in the street a moment, in the glare of the red light, before he faded into darkness. Without knowing exactly why, Kane had an instinct that the stranger knew no one in San Francisco, and after leaving the shop was going into utter silence and obscurity.

A few moments later Dr. Sparlow returned to relieve his wearied partner. A pushing, active man, he listened impatiently to Kane's account of his youthful practice with Madame le Blanc, without, however, dwelling much on his methods. "You ought to have charged her more," the elder said decisively. "She'd have paid it. She only came here because she was ashamed to go to a big shop in Montgomery Street—and she won't come again."

"But she wants you to see her to-morrow," urged Kane, "and I told her you would!"

"You say it was only a superficial cut?" queried the doctor, "and you closed it? Umph! what can she want to see ME for?" He paid more attention, however, to the case of the stranger, Allen. "When he comes here again, manage to let me see him." Mr. Kane promised, yet for some indefinable reason he went home that night not quite as well satisfied with himself.

He was much more concerned the next morning when, after relieving the doctor for his regular morning visits, he was startled an hour later by the abrupt return of that gentleman. His face was marked by some excitement and anxiety, which nevertheless struggled with that sense of the ludicrous which Californians in those days imported into most situations of perplexity or catastrophe. Putting his hands deeply into his trousers pockets, he confronted his youthful partner behind the counter.

"How much did you charge that French-woman?" he said gravely.

"Twenty-five cents," said Kane timidly.

"Well, I'd give it back and add two hundred and fifty dollars if she had never entered the shop."

"What's the matter?"

"Her head will be—and a mass of it, in a day, I reckon! Why, man, you put enough plaster on it to clothe and paper the dome of the Capitol! You drew her scalp together so that she couldn't shut her eyes without climbing up the bed-post! You mowed her hair off so that she'll have to wear a wig for the next two years—and handed it to her in a beau-ti-ful sealed package! They talk of suing me and killing you out of hand."

"She was bleeding a great deal and looked faint," said the junior partner; "I thought I ought to stop that."

"And you did—by thunder! Though it might have been better business for the shop if I'd found her a crumbling ruin here, than lathed and plastered in this fashion, over there! However," he added, with a laugh, seeing an angry light in his junior partner's eye, "SHE don't seem to mind it—the cursing all comes from THEM. SHE rather likes your style and praises it—that's what gets me! Did you talk to her much," he added, looking critically at his partner.

"I only told her to sit still or she'd bleed to death," said Kane curtly.

"Humph!—she jabbered something about your being 'strong' and knowing just how to handle her. Well, it can't be helped now. I think I came in time for the worst of it and have drawn their fire. Don't do it again. The next time a woman with a cut head and long hair tackles you, fill up her scalp with lint and tannin, and pack her off to some of the big shops and make THEM pick it out." And with a good-humored nod he started off to finish his interrupted visits.

With a vague sense of remorse, and yet a consciousness of some injustice done him, Mr. Kane resumed his occupation with filters and funnels, and mortars and triturations. He was so gloomily preoccupied that he did not, as usual, glance out of the window, or he would have observed the mining stranger of the previous night before it. It was not until the man's bowed shoulders blocked the light of the doorway that he looked up and recognized him. Kane was in no mood to welcome his appearance. His presence, too, actively recalled the last night's adventure of which he was a witness—albeit a sympathizing one. Kane shrank from the illusions which he felt he would be sure to make. And with his present ill luck, he was by no means sure that his ministrations even to HIM had been any more successful than they had been to the Frenchwoman. But a glance at his good-humored face and kindling eyes removed that suspicion. Nevertheless, he felt somewhat embarrassed and impatient, and perhaps could not entirely conceal it. He forgot that the rudest natures are sometimes the most delicately sensitive to slights, and the stranger had noticed his manner and began apologetically.

"I allowed I'd just drop in anyway to tell ye that these thar pills you giv' me did me a heap o' good so far—though mebbe it's only fair to give the others a show too, which I'm reckoning to do." He paused, and then in a submissive confidence went on: "But first I wanted to hev you excuse me for havin' asked all them questions about that high-toned lady last night, when it warn't none of my business. I am a darned fool."

Mr. Kane instantly saw that it was no use to keep up his attitude of secrecy, or impose upon the ignorant, simple man, and said hurriedly: "Oh no. The lady is very well known. She is the proprietress of a restaurant down the street—a house open to everybody. Her name is Madame le Blanc; you may have heard of her before?"

To his surprise the man exhibited no diminution of interest nor change of sentiment at this intelligence. "Then," he said slowly, "I reckon I might get to see her again. Ye see, Mr. Kane, I rather took a fancy to her general style and gait—arter seein' her in that fix last night. It was rather like them play pictures on the stage. Ye don't think she'd make any fuss to seein' a rough old 'forty-niner' like me?"

"Hardly," said Kane, "but there might be some objection from her gentlemen friends," he added, with a smile,—"Jack Lane, a gambler, who keeps a faro bank in her rooms, and Jimmy O'Ryan, a prize-fighter, who is one of her 'chuckers out.'"

His further relation of Madame le Blanc's entourage apparently gave the miner no concern. He looked at Kane, nodded, and repeated slowly and appreciatively: "Yes, keeps a gamblin' and faro bank and a prize-fighter—I reckon that might be about her gait and style too. And you say she lives"—

He stopped, for at this moment a man entered the shop quickly, shut the door behind him, and turned the key in the lock. It was done so quickly that Kane instinctively felt that the man had been loitering in the vicinity and had approached from the side street. A single glance at the intruder's face and figure showed him that it was the bully of whom he had just spoken. He had seen that square, brutal face once before, confronting the police in a riot, and had not forgotten it. But today, with the flush of liquor on it, it had an impatient awkwardness and confused embarrassment that he could not account for. He did not comprehend that the genuine bully is seldom deliberate of attack, and is obliged—in common with many of the combative lower animals—to lash himself into a previous fury of provocation. This probably saved him, as perhaps some instinctive feeling that he was in no immediate danger kept him cool. He remained standing quietly behind the counter. Allen glanced around carelessly, looking at the shelves.

The silence of the two men apparently increased the ruffian's rage and embarrassment. Suddenly he leaped into the air with a whoop and clumsily executed a negro double shuffle on the floor, which jarred the glasses—yet was otherwise so singularly ineffective and void of purpose that he stopped in the midst of it and had to content himself with glaring at Kane.

"Well," said Kane quietly, "what does all this mean? What do you want here?"

"What does it mean?" repeated the bully, finding his voice in a high falsetto, designed to imitate Kane's. "It means I'm going to play merry h-ll with this shop! It means I'm goin' to clean it out and the blank hair-cuttin' blank that keeps it. What do I want here? Well—what I want I intend to help myself to, and all h-ll can't stop me! And" (working himself to the striking point) "who the blank are you to ask me?" He sprang towards the counter, but at the same moment Allen seemed to slip almost imperceptibly and noiselessly between them, and Kane found himself confronted only by the miner's broad back.

"Hol' yer hosses, stranger," said Allen slowly, as the ruffian suddenly collided with his impassive figure. "I'm a sick man comin' in yer for medicine. I've got somethin' wrong with my heart, and goin's on like this yer kinder sets it to thumpin'."

"Blank you and your blank heart!" screamed the bully, turning in a fury of amazement and contempt at this impotent interruption. "Who"—but his voice stopped. Allen's power-ful right arm had passed over his head and shoulders like a steel hoop, and pinioned his elbows against his sides. Held rigidly upright, he attempted to kick, but Allen's right leg here advanced, and firmly held his lower limbs against the counter that shook to his struggles and blasphemous outcries. Allen turned quietly to Kane, and, with a gesture of his unemployed arm, said confidentially:

"Would ye mind passing me down that ar Romantic Spirits of Ammonyer ye gave me last night?"

Kane caught the idea, and handed him the bottle.

"Thar," said Allen, taking out the stopper and holding the pungent spirit against the bully's dilated nostrils and vociferous mouth, "thar, smell that, and taste it, it will do ye good; it was powerful kammin' to ME last night."

The ruffian gasped, coughed, choked, but his blaspheming voice died away in a suffocating hiccough.

"Thar," continued Allen, as his now subdued captive relaxed his struggling, "ye 'r' better, and so am I. It's quieter here now, and ye ain't affectin' my heart so bad. A little fresh air will make us both all right." He turned again to Kane in his former subdued confidential manner.

"Would ye mind openin' that door?"

Kane flew to the door, unlocked it, and held it wide open. The bully again began to struggle, but a second inhalation of the hartshorn quelled him, and enabled his captor to drag him to the door. As they emerged upon the sidewalk, the bully, with a final desperate struggle, freed his arm and grasped his pistol at his hip-pocket, but at the same moment Allen deliberately caught his hand, and with a powerful side throw cast him on the pavement, retaining the weapon in his own hand. "I've one of my own," he said to the prostrate man, "but I reckon I'll keep this yer too, until you're better."

The crowd that had collected quickly, recognizing the notorious and discomfited bully, were not of a class to offer him any sympathy, and he slunk away followed by their jeers. Allen returned quietly to the shop. Kane was profuse in his thanks, and yet oppressed with his simple friend's fatuous admiration for a woman who could keep such ruffians in her employ. "You know who that man was, I suppose?" he said.

"I reckon it was that 'er prize-fighter belongin' to that high-toned lady," returned Allen simply. "But he don't know anything about RASTLIN', b'gosh; only that I was afraid o' bringin' on that heart trouble, I mout hev hurt him bad."

"They think"—hesitated Kane, "that—I—was rough in my treatment of that woman and maliciously cut off her hair. This attack was revenge—or"—he hesitated still more, as he remembered Dr. Sparlow's indication of the woman's feeling—"or that bully's idea of revenge."

"I see," nodded Allen, opening his small sympathetic eyes on Kane with an exasperating air of secrecy—"just jealousy."

Kane reddened in sheer hopelessness of explanation. "No; it was earning his wages, as he thought."

"Never ye mind, pard," said Allen confidentially. "I'll set 'em both right. Ye see, this sorter gives me a show to call at that thar restaurant and give HIM back his six-shooter, and set her on the right trail for you. Why, Lordy! I was here when you was fixin' her—I'm testimony o' the way you did it—and she'll remember me. I'll sorter waltz round thar this afternoon. But I reckon I won't be keepin' YOU from your work any longer. And look yar!—I say, pard!—this is seein'

Bret Harte

life in 'Frisco—ain't it? Gosh! I've had more high times in this very shop in two days, than I've had in two years of St. Jo. So long, Mr. Kane!" He waved his hand, lounged slowly out of the shop, gave a parting glance up the street, passed the window, and was gone.

The next day being a half-holiday for Kane, he did not reach the shop until afternoon. "Your mining friend Allen has been here," said Doctor Sparlow. "I took the liberty of introducing myself, and induced him to let me carefully examine him. He was a little shy, and I am sorry for it, as I fear he has some serious organic trouble with his heart and ought to have a more thorough examination." Seeing Kane's unaffected concern, he added, "You might influence him to do so. He's a good fellow and ought to take some care of himself. By the way, he told me to tell you that he'd seen Madame le Blanc and made it all right about you. He seems to be quite infatuated with the woman."

"I'm sorry he ever saw her," said Kane bitterly.

"Well, his seeing her seems to have saved the shop from being smashed up, and you from getting a punched head," returned the Doctor with a laugh. "He's no fool—yet it's a freak of human nature that a simple hayseed like that—a man who's lived in the backwoods all his life, is likely to be the first to tumble before a pot of French rouge like her."

Indeed, in a couple of weeks, there was no further doubt of Mr. Reuben Allen's infatuation. He dropped into the shop frequently on his way to and from the restaurant, where he now regularly took his meals; he spent his evenings in gambling in its private room. Yet Kane was by no means sure that he was losing his money there unfairly, or that he was used as a pigeon by the proprietress and her friends. The bully O'Ryan was turned away; Sparlow grimly suggested that Allen had simply taken his place, but Kane ingeniously retorted that the Doctor was only piqued because Allen had evaded his professional treatment. Certainly the patient had never consented to another examination, although he repeatedly and gravely bought medicines, and was a generous customer. Once or twice Kane thought it his duty to caution Allen against his new friends and enlighten him as to Madame le Blanc's reputation, but his suggestions were received with a good-humored submission that was either the effect of unbelief or of perfect resignation to the fact, and he desisted. One morning Dr. Sparlow said cheerfully:—

"Would you like to hear the last thing about your friend and the Frenchwoman? The boys can't account for her singling out a fellow like that for her friend, so they say that the night that she cut herself at the fete and dropped in here for assistance, she found nobody here but Allen—a chance customer! That it was HE who cut off her hair and bound up her wounds in that sincere fashion, and she believed he had saved her life." The Doctor grinned maliciously as he added: "And as that's the way history is written you see your reputation is safe."

It may have been a month later that San Francisco was thrown into a paroxysm of horror and indignation over the assassination of a prominent citizen and official in the gambling-rooms of Madame le Blanc, at the hands of a notorious gambler. The gambler had escaped, but in one of those rare spasms of vengeful morality which sometimes overtakes communities who have too long winked at and suffered the existence of evil, the fair proprietress and her whole entourage were arrested and haled before the coroner's jury at the inquest. The greatest excitement prevailed; it was said that if the jury failed in their duty, the Vigilance Committee had arranged for the destruction of the establishment and the deportation of its inmates. The crowd that had collected around the building was reinforced by Kane and Dr. Sparlow, who had closed their shop in the next block to attend. When Kane had fought his way into the building and the temporary court, held in the splendidly furnished gambling saloon, whose gilded mirrors reflected the eager faces of the crowd, the Chief of Police was giving his testimony in a formal official manner, impressive only for its relentless and impassive revelation of the character and antecedents of the proprietress. The house had been long under the espionage of the police; Madame le Blanc had a dozen aliases; she was "wanted" in New Orleans, in New York, in Havana! It was in HER house that Dyer, the bank clerk, committed suicide; it was there that Colonel Hooley was set upon by her bully, O'Ryan; it was she—Kane heard with reddening cheeks—who defied the police with riotous conduct at a fete two months ago. As he coolly recited the counts of this shameful indictment, Kane looked eagerly around for Allen, whom he knew had been arrested as a witness. How would HE take this terrible disclosure? He was sitting with the others, his arm thrown over the back of his chair, and his good-humored face turned towards the woman, in his old confidential attitude. SHE, gorgeously dressed, painted, but unblushing, was cool, collected, and cynical.

The Coroner next called the only witness of the actual tragedy, "Reuben Allen." The man did not move nor change his position. The summons was repeated; a policeman touched him on the shoulder. There was a pause, and the officer announced: "He has fainted, your Honor!"

"Is there a physician present?" asked the Coroner.

Sparlow edged his way quickly to the front. "I'm a medical man," he said to the Coroner, as he passed quickly to the still, upright, immovable figure and knelt beside it with his head upon his heart. There was an awed silence as, after a pause, he rose slowly to his feet.

"The witness is a patient, your Honor, whom I examined some weeks ago and found suffering from valvular disease of the heart. He is dead."

THREE VAGABONDS OF TRINIDAD

"Oh! it's you, is it?" said the Editor.

The Chinese boy to whom the colloquialism was addressed answered literally, after his habit:—

"Allee same Li Tee; me no changee. Me no ollee China boy."

"That's so," said the Editor with an air of conviction. "I don't suppose there's another imp like you in all Trinidad County. Well, next time don't scratch outside there like a gopher, but come in."

"Lass time," suggested Li Tee blandly, "me tap tappee. You no like tap tappee. You say, alle same dam woodpeckel."

It was quite true—the highly sylvan surroundings of the Trinidad "Sentinel" office—a little clearing in a pine forest—and its attendant fauna, made these signals confusing. An accurate imitation of a woodpecker was also one of Li Tee's accomplishments.

The Editor without replying finished the note he was writing; at which Li Tee, as if struck by some coincident recollection, lifted up his long sleeve, which served him as a pocket, and carelessly shook out a letter on the table like a conjuring trick. The Editor, with a reproachful glance at him, opened it. It was only the ordinary request of an agricultural subscriber —one Johnson—that the Editor would "notice" a giant radish grown by the subscriber and sent by the bearer.

"Where's the radish, Li Tee?" said the Editor suspiciously.

"No hab got. Ask Mellikan boy."

"What?"

Here Li Tee condescended to explain that on passing the schoolhouse he had been set upon by the schoolboys, and that in the struggle the big radish—being, like most such monstrosities of the quick Californian soil, merely a mass of organized water—was "mashed" over the head of some of his assailants. The Editor, painfully aware of these regular persecutions of his errand boy, and perhaps realizing that a radish which could not be used as a bludgeon was not of a sustaining nature, forebore any reproof. "But I cannot notice what I haven't seen, Li Tee," he said good-humoredly.

"S'pose you lie—allee same as Johnson," suggested Li with equal cheerfulness. "He foolee you with lotten stuff—you foolee Mellikan man, allee same."

The Editor preserved a dignified silence until he had addressed his letter. "Take this to Mrs. Martin," he said, handing it to the boy; "and mind you keep clear of the schoolhouse. Don't go by the Flat either if the men are at work, and don't, if you value your skin, pass Flanigan's shanty, where you set off those firecrackers and nearly burnt him out the other day. Look out for Barker's dog at the crossing, and keep off the main road if the tunnel men are coming over the hill." Then remembering that he had virtually closed all the ordinary approaches to Mrs. Martin's house, he added, "Better go round by the woods, where you won't meet ANY ONE."

The boy darted off through the open door, and the Editor stood for a moment looking regretfully after him. He liked his little protege ever since that unfortunate child—a waif from a Chinese wash-house—was impounded by some indignant miners for bringing home a highly imperfect and insufficient washing, and kept as hostage for a more proper return of the garments. Unfortunately, another gang of miners, equally aggrieved, had at the same time looted the wash-house and driven off the occupants, so that Li Tee remained unclaimed. For a few weeks he became a sporting appendage of the miners' camp; the stolid butt of good-humored practical jokes, the victim alternately of careless indifference or of extravagant generosity. He received kicks and half-dollars intermittently, and pocketed both with stoical fortitude. But under this treatment he presently lost the docility and frugality which was part of his inheritance, and began to put his small wits against his tormentors, until they grew tired of their own mischief and his. But they knew not what to do with him. His pretty nankeen-yellow skin debarred him from the white "public school," while, although as a heathen he might have reasonably claimed attention from the Sabbath-school, the parents who cheerfully gave their contributions to the heathen ABROAD, objected to him as a companion of their children in the church at home. At this juncture the Editor offered to take him into his printing office as a "devil." For a while he seemed to be endeavoring, in his old literal way, to act up to that title. He inked everything but the press. He scratched Chinese characters of an abusive import on "leads," printed them, and stuck them about the office; he put "punk" in the foreman's pipe, and had been seen to swallow small type merely as a diabolical recreation. As a messenger he was fleet of foot, but uncertain of delivery. Some time previously the Editor had enlisted the sympathies of Mrs. Martin, the good-natured wife of a farmer, to take him in her household on trial, but on the third day Li Tee had run away. Yet the Editor had not despaired, and it was to urge her to a second attempt that he dispatched that letter.

He was still gazing abstractedly into the depths of the wood when he was conscious of a slight movement—but no sound—in a clump of hazel near him, and a stealthy figure glided from it. He at once recognized it as "Jim," a well-known drunken Indian vagrant of the settlement—tied to its civilization by the single link of "fire water," for which he forsook equally the Reservation where it was forbidden and his own camps where it was unknown. Unconscious of his silent observer, he dropped upon all fours, with his ear and nose alternately to the ground like some tracking animal. Then having satisfied himself, he rose, and bending forward in a dogged trot, made a straight line for the woods. He was followed a few seconds later by his dog—a slinking, rough, wolf-like brute, whose superior instinct, however, made him detect the silent presence of some alien humanity in the person of the Editor, and to recognize it with a yelp of habit, anticipatory of the stone that he knew was always thrown at him.

"That's cute," said a voice, "but it's just what I expected all along."

The Editor turned quickly. His foreman was standing behind him, and had evidently noticed the whole incident.

"It's what I allus said," continued the man. "That boy and that Injin are thick as thieves. Ye can't see one without the other—and they've got their little tricks and signals by which they follow each other. T'other day when you was kalkilatin'

Bret Harte

Li Tee was doin' your errands I tracked him out on the marsh, just by followin' that ornery, pizenous dog o' Jim's. There was the whole caboodle of 'em—including Jim—campin' out, and eatin' raw fish that Jim had ketched, and green stuff they had both sneaked outer Johnson's garden. Mrs. Martin may TAKE him, but she won't keep him long while Jim's round. What makes Li foller that blamed old Injin soaker, and what makes Jim, who, at least, is a 'Merican, take up with a furrin' heathen, just gets me."

The Editor did not reply. He had heard something of this before. Yet, after all, why should not these equal outcasts of civilization cling together!

*****

Li Tee's stay with Mrs. Martin was brief. His departure was hastened by an untoward event—apparently ushered in, as in the case of other great calamities, by a mysterious portent in the sky. One morning an extraordinary bird of enormous dimensions was seen approaching from the horizon, and eventually began to hover over the devoted town. Careful scrutiny of this ominous fowl, however, revealed the fact that it was a monstrous Chinese kite, in the shape of a flying dragon. The spectacle imparted considerable liveliness to the community, which, however, presently changed to some concern and indignation. It appeared that the kite was secretly constructed by Li Tee in a secluded part of Mrs. Martin's clearing, but when it was first tried by him he found that through some error of design it required a tail of unusual proportions. This he hurriedly supplied by the first means he found—Mrs. Martin's clothes-line, with part of the weekly wash depending from it. This fact was not at first noticed by the ordinary sightseer, although the tail seemed peculiar—yet, perhaps, not more peculiar than a dragon's tail ought to be. But when the actual theft was discovered and reported through the town, a vivacious interest was created, and spy-glasses were used to identify the various articles of apparel still hanging on that ravished clothes-line. These garments, in the course of their slow disengagement from the clothes-pins through the gyrations of the kite, impartially distributed themselves over the town—one of Mrs. Martin's stockings falling upon the veranda of the Polka Saloon, and the other being afterwards discovered on the belfry of the First Methodist Church—to the scandal of the congregation. It would have been well if the result of Li Tee's invention had ended here. Alas! the kite-flyer and his accomplice, "Injin Jim," were tracked by means of the kite's tell-tale cord to a lonely part of the marsh and rudely dispossessed of their charge by Deacon Hornblower and a constable. Unfortunately, the captors overlooked the fact that the kite-flyers had taken the precaution of making a "half-turn" of the stout cord around a log to ease the tremendous pull of the kite—whose power the captors had not reckoned upon—and the Deacon incautiously substituted his own body for the log. A singular spectacle is said to have then presented itself to the on-lookers. The Deacon was seen to be running wildly by leaps and bounds over the marsh after the kite, closely followed by the constable in equally wild efforts to restrain him by tugging at the end of the line. The extraordinary race continued to the town until the constable fell, losing his hold of the line. This seemed to impart a singular specific levity to the Deacon, who, to the astonishment of everybody, incontinently sailed up into a tree! When he was succored and cut down from the demoniac kite, he was found to have sustained a dislocation of the shoulder, and the constable was severely shaken. By that one infelicitous stroke the two outcasts made an enemy of the Law and the Gospel as represented in Trinidad County. It is to be feared also that the ordinary emotional instinct of a frontier community, to which they were now simply abandoned, was as little to be trusted. In this dilemma they disappeared from the town the next day—no one knew where. A pale blue smoke rising from a lonely island in the bay for some days afterwards suggested their possible refuge. But nobody greatly cared. The sympathetic mediation of the Editor was characteristically opposed by Mr. Parkin Skinner, a prominent citizen:—

"It's all very well for you to talk sentiment about niggers, Chinamen, and Injins, and you fellers can laugh about the Deacon being snatched up to heaven like Elijah in that blamed Chinese chariot of a kite—but I kin tell you, gentlemen, that this is a white man's country! Yes, sir, you can't get over it! The nigger of every description—yeller, brown, or black, call him 'Chinese,' 'Injin,' or 'Kanaka,' or what you like—hez to clar off of God's footstool when the Anglo-Saxon gets started! It stands to reason that they can't live alongside o' printin' presses, M'Cormick's reapers, and the Bible! Yes, sir! the Bible; and Deacon Hornblower kin prove it to you. It's our manifest destiny to clar them out—that's what we was put here for—and it's just the work we've got to do!"

I have ventured to quote Mr. Skinner's stirring remarks to show that probably Jim and Li Tee ran away only in anticipation of a possible lynching, and to prove that advanced sentiments of this high and ennobling nature really obtained forty years ago in an ordinary American frontier town which did not then dream of Expansion and Empire!

Howbeit, Mr. Skinner did not make allowance for mere human nature. One morning Master Bob Skinner, his son, aged twelve, evaded the schoolhouse, and started in an old Indian "dug-out" to invade the island of the miserable refugees. His purpose was not clearly defined to himself, but was to be modified by circumstances. He would either capture Li Tee and Jim, or join them in their lawless existence. He had prepared himself for either event by surreptitiously borrowing his father's gun. He also carried victuals, having heard that Jim ate grasshoppers and Li Tee rats, and misdoubting his own capacity for either diet. He paddled slowly, well in shore, to be secure from observation at home, and then struck out boldly in his leaky canoe for the island—a tufted, tussocky shred of the marshy promontory torn off in some tidal storm. It was a lovely day, the bay being barely ruffled by the afternoon "trades;" but as he neared the island he came upon the swell from the bar and the thunders of the distant Pacific, and grew a little frightened. The canoe, losing way, fell into the trough of the swell, shipping salt water, still more alarming to the prairie-bred boy. Forgetting his plan of a stealthy invasion, he shouted lustily as the helpless and water-logged boat began to drift past the island; at which a lithe figure emerged from the reeds, threw off a tattered blanket, and slipped noiselessly, like some animal, into the water. It was Jim, who, half wading, half swimming, brought the canoe and boy ashore. Master Skinner at once gave up the idea of invasion, and concluded to join the refugees.

This was easy in his defenceless state, and his manifest delight in their rude encampment and gypsy life, although he had been one of Li Tee's oppressors in the past. But that stolid pagan had a philosophical indifference which might have passed for Christian forgiveness, and Jim's native reticence seemed like assent. And, possibly, in the minds of these two vagabonds there might have been a natural sympathy for this other truant from civilization, and some delicate flattery in the fact that Master Skinner was not driven out, but came of his own accord. Howbeit, they fished together, gathered cranberries on the marsh, shot a wild duck and two plovers, and when Master Skinner assisted in the cooking of their fish in a conical basket sunk in the ground, filled with water, heated by rolling red-hot stones from their drift-wood fire into the buried basket, the boy's felicity was supreme. And what an afternoon! To lie, after this feast, on their bellies in the grass, replete like animals, hidden from everything but the sunshine above them; so quiet that gray clouds of sandpipers settled fearlessly around them, and a shining brown muskrat slipped from the ooze within a few feet of their faces—was to feel themselves a part of the wild life in earth and sky. Not that their own predatory instincts were hushed by this divine peace; that intermitting black spot upon the water, declared by the Indian to be a seal, the stealthy glide of a yellow fox in the ambush of a callow brood of mallards, the momentary straying of an elk from the upland upon the borders of the marsh, awoke their tingling nerves to the happy but fruitless chase. And when night came, too soon, and they pigged together around the warm ashes of their camp-fire, under the low lodge poles of their wigwam of dried mud, reeds, and driftwood, with the combined odors of fish, wood-smoke, and the warm salt breath of the marsh in their nostrils, they slept contentedly. The distant lights of the settlement went out one by one, the stars came out, very large and very silent, to take their places. The barking of a dog on the nearest point was followed by another farther inland. But Jim's dog, curled at the feet of his master, did not reply. What had HE to do with civilization?

The morning brought some fear of consequences to Master Skinner, but no abatement of his resolve not to return. But here he was oddly combated by Li Tee. "S'pose you go back allee same. You tellee fam'lee canoe go topside down—you plentee swimee to bush. Allee night in bush. Housee big way off—how can get? Sabe?"

"And I'll leave the gun, and tell Dad that when the canoe upset the gun got drowned," said the boy eagerly.

Li Tee nodded.

"And come again Saturday, and bring more powder and shot and a bottle for Jim," said Master Skinner excitedly.

"Good!" grunted the Indian.

Then they ferried the boy over to the peninsula, and set him on a trail across the marshes, known only to themselves, which would bring him home. And when the Editor the next morning chronicled among his news, "Adrift on the Bay—A Schoolboy's Miraculous Escape," he knew as little what part his missing Chinese errand boy had taken in it as the rest of his readers.

Meantime the two outcasts returned to their island camp. It may have occurred to them that a little of the sunlight had gone from it with Bob; for they were in a dull, stupid way fascinated by the little white tyrant who had broken bread with them. He had been delightfully selfish and frankly brutal to them, as only a schoolboy could be, with the addition of the consciousness of his superior race. Yet they each longed for his return, although he was seldom mentioned in their scanty conversation—carried on in monosyllables, each in his own language, or with some common English word, or more often restricted solely to signs. By a delicate flattery, when they did speak of him it was in what they considered to be his own language.

"Boston boy, plenty like catchee HIM," Jim would say, pointing to a distant swan. Or Li Tee, hunting a striped water snake from the reeds, would utter stolidly, "Melikan boy no likee snake." Yet the next two days brought some trouble and physical discomfort to them. Bob had consumed, or wasted, all their provisions—and, still more unfortunately, his righteous visit, his gun, and his superabundant animal spirits had frightened away the game, which their habitual quiet and taciturnity had beguiled into trustfulness. They were half starved, but they did not blame him. It would come all right when he returned. They counted the days, Jim with secret notches on the long pole, Li Tee with a string of copper "cash" he always kept with him. The eventful day came at last,—a warm autumn day, patched with inland fog like blue smoke and smooth, tranquil, open surfaces of wood and sea; but to their waiting, confident eyes the boy came not out of either. They kept a stolid silence all that day until night fell, when Jim said, "Mebbe Boston boy go dead." Li Tee nodded. It did not seem possible to these two heathens that anything else could prevent the Christian child from keeping his word.

After that, by the aid of the canoe, they went much on the marsh, hunting apart, but often meeting on the trail which Bob had taken, with grunts of mutual surprise. These suppressed feelings, never made known by word or gesture, at last must have found vicarious outlet in the taciturn dog, who so far forgot his usual discretion as to once or twice seat himself on the water's edge and indulge in a fit of howling. It had been a custom of Jim's on certain days to retire to some secluded place, where, folded in his blanket, with his back against a tree, he remained motionless for hours. In the settlement this had been usually referred to the after effects of drink, known as the "horrors," but Jim had explained it by saying it was "when his heart was bad." And now it seemed, by these gloomy abstractions, that "his heart was bad" very often. And then the long withheld rains came one night on the wings of a fierce southwester, beating down their frail lodge and scattering it abroad, quenching their camp-fire, and rolling up the bay until it invaded their reedy island and hissed in their ears. It drove the game from Jim's gun; it tore the net and scattered the bait of Li Tee, the fisherman. Cold and half starved in heart and body, but more dogged and silent than ever, they crept out in their canoe into the storm-tossed bay, barely escaping with their miserable lives to the marshy peninsula. Here, on their enemy's ground, skulking in the rushes, or lying close behind tussocks, they at last reached the fringe of forest below the settlement. Here, too, sorely pressed by hunger, and doggedly reckless of consequences, they forgot their caution, and a flight of teal fell to Jim's gun on the very outskirts of the settlement.

It was a fatal shot, whose echoes awoke the forces of civilization against them. For it was heard by a logger in his hut near the marsh, who, looking out, had seen Jim pass. A careless, good-natured frontiersman, he might have kept the outcasts' mere presence to himself; but there was that damning shot! An Indian with a gun! That weapon, contraband of law, with dire fines and penalties to whoso sold or gave it to him! A thing to be looked into—some one to be punished! An Indian with a weapon that made him the equal of the white! Who was safe? He hurried to town to lay his information before the constable, but, meeting Mr. Skinner, imparted the news to him. The latter pooh-poohed the constable, who he alleged had not yet discovered the whereabouts of Jim, and suggested that a few armed citizens should make the chase themselves. The fact was that Mr. Skinner, never quite satisfied in his mind with his son's account of the loss of the gun, had put two and two together, and was by no means inclined to have his own gun possibly identified by the legal authority. Moreover, he went home and at once attacked Master Bob with such vigor and so highly colored a description of the crime he had committed, and the penalties attached to it, that Bob confessed. More than that, I grieve to say that Bob lied. The Indian had "stoled his gun," and threatened his life if he divulged the theft. He told how he was ruthlessly put ashore, and compelled to take a trail only known to them to reach his home. In two hours it was reported throughout the settlement that the infamous Jim had added robbery with violence to his illegal possession of the weapon. The secret of the island and the trail over the marsh was told only to a few.

Meantime it had fared hard with the fugitives. Their nearness
to the settlement prevented them from lighting a fire, which
might have revealed their hiding-place, and they crept
together, shivering all night in a clump of hazel. Scared
thence by passing but unsuspecting wayfarers wandering off
the trail, they lay part of the next day and night amid some
tussocks of salt grass, blown on by the cold sea-breeze;
chilled, but securely hidden from sight. Indeed, thanks to
some mysterious power they had of utter immobility, it was
wonderful how they could efface themselves, through quiet
and the simplest environment. The lee side of a straggling
vine in the meadow, or even the thin ridge of cast-up drift on
the shore, behind which they would lie for hours motionless,
was a sufficient barrier against prying eyes. In this
occupation they no longer talked together, but followed each
other with the blind instinct of animals—yet always
unerringly, as if conscious of each other's plans. Strangely
enough, it was the REAL animal alone—their nameless
dog—who now betrayed impatience and a certain human
infirmity of temper. The concealment they were resigned to,
the sufferings they mutely accepted, he alone resented!
When certain scents or sounds, imperceptible to their senses,
were blown across their path, he would, with bristling back,
snarl himself into guttural and strangulated fury. Yet, in their
apathy, even this would have passed them unnoticed, but that
on the second night he disappeared suddenly, returning after
two hours' absence with bloody jaws—replete, but still
slinking and snappish. It was only in the morning that,
creeping on their hands and knees through the stubble, they
came upon the torn and mangled carcass of a sheep. The two
men looked at each other without speaking—they knew what
this act of rapine meant to themselves. It meant a fresh hue
and cry after them—it meant that their starving companion
had helped to draw the net closer round them. The Indian

grunted, Li Tee smiled vacantly; but with their knives and fingers they finished what the dog had begun, and became equally culpable. But that they were heathens, they could not have achieved a delicate ethical responsibility in a more Christian-like way.

Yet the rice-fed Li Tee suffered most in their privations. His habitual apathy increased with a certain physical lethargy which Jim could not understand. When they were apart he sometimes found Li Tee stretched on his back with an odd stare in his eyes, and once, at a distance, he thought he saw a vague thin vapor drift from where the Chinese boy was lying and vanish as he approached. When he tried to arouse him there was a weak drawl in his voice and a drug-like odor in his breath. Jim dragged him to a more substantial shelter, a thicket of alder. It was dangerously near the frequented road, but a vague idea had sprung up in Jim's now troubled mind that, equal vagabonds though they were, Li Tee had more claims upon civilization, through those of his own race who were permitted to live among the white men, and were not hunted to "reservations" and confined there like Jim's people. If Li Tee was "heap sick," other Chinamen might find and nurse him. As for Li Tee, he had lately said, in a more lucid interval: "Me go dead—allee samee Mellikan boy. You go dead too—allee samee," and then lay down again with a glassy stare in his eyes. Far from being frightened at this, Jim attributed his condition to some enchantment that Li Tee had evoked from one of his gods—just as he himself had seen "medicine-men" of his own tribe fall into strange trances, and was glad that the boy no longer suffered. The day advanced, and Li Tee still slept. Jim could hear the church bells ringing; he knew it was Sunday—the day on which he was hustled from the main street by the constable; the day on which the shops were closed, and the drinking saloons open only at the back door. The day whereon no man worked—and for that reason, though he knew it not, the day selected by the ingenious Mr. Skinner and a few friends as especially fitting and convenient for a chase of the fugitives. The bell brought no suggestion of this—though the dog snapped under his breath and stiffened his spine. And then he heard another sound, far off and vague, yet one that brought a flash into his murky eye, that lit up the heaviness of his Hebraic face, and even showed a slight color in his high cheek-bones. He lay down on the ground, and listened with suspended breath. He heard it now distinctly. It was the Boston boy calling, and the word he was calling was "Jim."

Then the fire dropped out of his eyes as he turned with his usual stolidity to where Li Tee was lying. Him he shook, saying briefly: "Boston boy come back!" But there was no reply, the dead body rolled over inertly under his hand; the head fell back, and the jaw dropped under the pinched yellow face. The Indian gazed at him slowly, and then gravely turned again in the direction of the voice. Yet his dull mind was perplexed, for, blended with that voice were other sounds like the tread of clumsily stealthy feet. But again the voice called "Jim!" and raising his hands to his lips he gave a low whoop in reply. This was followed by silence, when suddenly he heard the voice—the boy's voice—once again, this time very near him, saying eagerly:—

"There he is!"

Then the Indian knew all. His face, however, did not change as he took up his gun, and a man stepped out of the thicket into the trail:—

"Drop that gun, you d—d Injin."

The Indian did not move.

"Drop it, I say!"

The Indian remained erect and motionless.

A rifle shot broke from the thicket. At first it seemed to have missed the Indian, and the man who had spoken cocked his own rifle. But the next moment the tall figure of Jim collapsed where he stood into a mere blanketed heap.

The man who had fired the shot walked towards the heap with the easy air of a conqueror. But suddenly there arose before him an awful phantom, the incarnation of savagery— a creature of blazing eyeballs, flashing tusks, and hot carnivorous breath. He had barely time to cry out "A wolf!" before its jaws met in his throat, and they rolled together on the ground.

But it was no wolf—as a second shot proved—only Jim's slinking dog; the only one of the outcasts who at that supreme moment had gone back to his original nature.

A VISION OF THE FOUNTAIN

Mr. Jackson Potter halted before the little cottage, half shop, half hostelry, opposite the great gates of Domesday Park, where tickets of admission to that venerable domain were sold. Here Mr. Potter revealed his nationality as a Western American, not only in his accent, but in a certain half-humorous, half-practical questioning of the ticket-seller—as that quasi-official stamped his ticket—which was nevertheless delivered with such unfailing good-humor, and such frank suggestiveness of the perfect equality of the ticket-seller and the well-dressed stranger that, far from producing any irritation, it attracted the pleased attention not only of the official, but his wife and daughter and a customer. Possibly the good looks of the stranger had something to do with it. Jackson Potter was a singularly handsome young fellow, with one of those ideal faces and figures sometimes seen in Western frontier villages, attributable to no ancestor, but evolved possibly from novels and books devoured by ancestresses in the long solitary winter evenings of their lonely cabins on the frontier. A beardless, classical head, covered by short flocculent blonde curls, poised on a shapely neck and shoulders, was more Greek in outline than suggestive of any ordinary American type. Finally, after having thoroughly amused his small audience, he lifted his straw hat to the "ladies," and lounged out across the road to the gateway. Here he paused, consulting his guide-book, and read aloud: "St. John's gateway. This massive structure, according to Leland, was built in"—murmured—"never mind when; we'll pass St. John," marked the page with his pencil, and tendering his ticket to the gate-keeper, heard, with some satisfaction, that, as there were no other visitors just then, and as the cicerone only accompanied PARTIES, he would be left to himself, and at once plunged into a by-path.

It was that loveliest of rare creations—a hot summer day in England, with all the dampness of that sea-blown isle wrung out of it, exhaled in the quivering blue vault overhead, or passing as dim wraiths in the distant wood, and all the long-matured growth of that great old garden vivified and made resplendent by the fervid sun. The ashes of dead and gone harvests, even the dust of those who had for ages wrought in it, turned again and again through incessant cultivation, seemed to move and live once more in that present sunshine. All color appeared to be deepened and mellowed, until even the very shadows of the trees were as velvety as the sward they fell upon. The prairie-bred Potter, accustomed to the youthful caprices and extravagances of his own virgin soil, could not help feeling the influence of the ripe restraints of this.

As he glanced through the leaves across green sunlit spaces to the ivy-clad ruins of Domesday Abbey, which seemed itself a growth of the very soil, he murmured to himself: "Things had been made mighty comfortable for folks here, you bet!" Forgotten books he had read as a boy, scraps of school histories, or rarer novels, came back to him as he walked along, and peopled the solitude about him with their heroes.

Nevertheless, it was unmistakably hot—a heat homelike in its intensity, yet of a different effect, throwing him into languid reverie rather than filling his veins with fire. Secure in his seclusion in the leafy chase, he took off his jacket and rambled on in his shirt sleeves. Through the opening he presently saw the abbey again, with the restored wing where the noble owner lived for two or three weeks in the year, but now given over to the prevailing solitude. And then, issuing from the chase, he came upon a broad, moss-grown terrace. Before him stretched a tangled and luxuriant wilderness of shrubs and flowers, darkened by cypress and cedars of Lebanon; its dun depths illuminated by dazzling white statues, vases, trellises, and paved paths, choked and lost in the trailing growths of years of abandonment and forget-fulness. He consulted his guide-book again. It was the "old Italian garden," constructed under the design of a famous Italian gardener by the third duke; but its studied formality being displeasing to his successor, it was allowed to fall into picturesque decay and negligent profusion, which were not, however, disturbed by later descendants,—a fact deplored by the artistic writer of the guide-book, who mournfully called attention to the rare beauty of the marble statues, urns, and fountains, ruined by neglect, although one or two of the rarer objects had been removed to Deep Dene Lodge, another seat of the present duke.

It is needless to say that Mr. Potter conceived at once a humorous opposition to the artistic enthusiasm of the critic, and, plunging into the garden, took a mischievous delight in its wildness and the victorious struggle of nature with the formality of art. At every step through the tangled labyrinth he could see where precision and order had been invaded, and even the rigid masonry broken or upheaved by the rebellious force. Yet here and there the two powers had combined to offer an example of beauty neither could have effected alone. A passion vine had overrun and enclasped a vase with a perfect symmetry no sculptor could have achieved. A heavy balustrade was made ethereal with a delicate fretwork of vegetation between its balusters like lace. Here, however, the lap and gurgle of water fell gratefully upon the ear of the perspiring and thirsty Mr. Potter, and turned his attention to more material things. Following the sound, he presently came upon an enormous oblong marble basin containing three time-worn fountains with grouped figures. The pipes were empty, silent, and choked with reeds and water plants, but the great basin itself was filled with water from some invisible source.

A terraced walk occupied one side of the long parallelogram; at intervals and along the opposite bank, half shadowed by willows, tinted marble figures of tritons, fauns, and dryads arose half hidden in the reeds. They were more or less mutilated by time, and here and there only the empty, moss-covered plinths that had once supported them could be seen. But they were so lifelike in their subdued color in the shade that he was for a moment startled.

The water looked deliciously cool. An audacious thought struck him. He was alone, and the place was a secluded one. He knew there were no other visitors; the marble basin was quite hidden from the rest of the garden, and approached only from the path by which he had come, and whose entire view he commanded. He quietly and deliberately undressed himself under the willows, and unhesitatingly plunged into the basin. The water was four or five feet deep, and its extreme length afforded an excellent swimming bath, despite the water-lilies and a few aquatic plants that mottled its clear surface, or the sedge that clung to the bases of the statues. He disported for some moments in the delicious element, and then seated himself upon one of the half-submerged plinths, almost hidden by reeds, that had once upheld a river god. Here, lazily resting himself upon his elbow, half his body still below the water, his quick ear was suddenly startled by a rustling noise and the sound of footsteps. For a moment he was inclined to doubt his senses; he could see only the empty path before him and the deserted terrace. But the sound became more distinct, and to his great uneasiness appeared to come from the OTHER side of the fringe of willows, where there was undoubtedly a path to the fountain which he had overlooked. His clothes were under those willows, but he was at least twenty yards from the bank and an equal distance from the terrace. He was about to slip beneath the water when, to his crowning horror, before he could do so, a young girl slowly appeared from the hidden willow path full upon the terrace. She was walking leisurely with a parasol over her head and a book in her hand. Even in his intense consternation her whole figure—a charming one in its white dress, sailor hat, and tan shoes—was imprinted on his memory as she instinctively halted to look upon the fountain, evidently an unexpected surprise to her.

A sudden idea flashed upon him. She was at least sixty yards away; he was half hidden in the reeds and well in the long shadows of the willows. If he remained perfectly motionless she might overlook him at that distance, or take him for one of the statues. He remembered also that as he was resting on his elbow, his half-submerged body lying on the plinth below water, he was somewhat in the attitude of one of the river gods. And there was no other escape. If he dived he might not be able to keep under water as long as she remained, and any movement he knew would betray him. He stiffened himself and scarcely breathed. Luckily for him his attitude had been a natural one and easy to keep. It was well, too, for she was evidently in no hurry and walked slowly, stopping from time to time to admire the basin and its figures. Suddenly he was instinctively aware that she was looking towards him and even changing her position, moving her pretty head and shading her eyes with her hand as if for a better view. He remained motionless, scarcely daring to breathe. Yet there was something so innocently frank and undisturbed in her observation, that he knew as instinctively that she suspected nothing, and took him for a half-submerged statue. He breathed more freely. But presently she stopped, glanced around her, and, keeping her eyes fixed in his direction, began to walk backwards slowly until she reached a stone balustrade behind her. On this she leaped, and, sitting down, opened in her lap the sketch-book she was carrying, and, taking out a pencil, to his horror began to sketch!

For a wild moment he recurred to his first idea of diving and swimming at all hazards to the bank, but the conviction that now his slightest movement must be detected held him motionless. He must save her the mortification of knowing she was sketching a living man, if he died for it. She sketched rapidly but fixedly and absorbedly, evidently forgetting all else in her work. From time to time she held out her sketch before her to compare it with her subject. Yet the seconds seemed minutes and the minutes hours. Suddenly, to his great relief, a distant voice was heard calling "Lottie." It was a woman's voice; by its accent it also seemed to him an American one.

The young girl made a slight movement of impatience, but did not look up, and her pencil moved still more rapidly. Again the voice called, this time nearer. The young girl's pencil fairly flew over the paper, as, still without looking up, she lifted a pretty voice and answered back, "Y-e-e-s!"

It struck him that her accent was also that of a compatriot.

"Where on earth are you?" continued the first voice, which now appeared to come from the other side of the willows on the path by which the young girl had approached. "Here, aunty," replied the girl, closing her sketch-book with a snap and starting to her feet.

A stout woman, fashionably dressed, made her appearance

Bret Harte

from the willow path.

"What have you been doing all this while?" she said querulously. "Not sketching, I hope," she added, with a suspicious glance at the book. "You know your professor expressly forbade you to do so in your holidays."

The young girl shrugged her shoulders. "I've been looking at the fountains," she replied evasively.

"And horrid looking pagan things they are, too," said the elder woman, turning from them disgustedly, without vouchsafing a second glance. "Come. If we expect to do the abbey, we must hurry up, or we won't catch the train. Your uncle is waiting for us at the top of the garden."

And, to Potter's intense relief, she grasped the young girl's arm and hurried her away, their figures the next moment vanishing in the tangled shrubbery.

Potter lost no time in plunging with his cramped limbs into the water and regaining the other side. Here he quickly half dried himself with some sun-warmed leaves and baked mosses, hurried on his clothes, and hastened off in the opposite direction to the path taken by them, yet with such circuitous skill and speed that he reached the great gateway without encountering anybody. A brisk walk brought him to the station in time to catch a stopping train, and in half an hour he was speeding miles away from Domesday Park and his half-forgotten episode.

*****

Meantime the two ladies continued on their way to the abbey. "I don't see why I mayn't sketch things I see about me," said the young lady impatiently. "Of course, I understand that I must go through the rudimentary drudgery of my art and study from casts, and learn perspective, and all that; but I can't see what's the difference between working in a stuffy studio over a hand or arm that I know is only a STUDY, and sketching a full or half length in the open air with the wonderful illusion of light and shade and distance—and grouping and combining them all—that one knows and feels makes a picture. The real picture one makes is already in one's self."

"For goodness' sake, Lottie, don't go on again with your usual absurdities. Since you are bent on being an artist, and your Popper has consented and put you under the most expensive master in Paris, the least you can do is to follow the rules. And I dare say he only wanted you to 'sink the shop' in company. It's such horrid bad form for you artistic people to be always dragging out your sketch-books. What would you say if your Popper came over here, and began to examine every lady's dress in society to see what material it was, just because he was a big dry-goods dealer in America?"

The young girl, accustomed to her aunt's extravagances, made no reply. But that night she consulted her sketch, and was so far convinced of her own instincts, and the profound impression the fountain had made upon her, that she was enabled to secretly finish her interrupted sketch from memory. For Miss Charlotte Forrest was a born artist, and in no mere caprice had persuaded her father to let her adopt the profession, and accepted the drudgery of a novitiate. She looked earnestly upon this first real work of her hand and found it good! Still, it was but a pencil sketch, and wanted the vivification of color.

When she returned to Paris she began—still secretly—a larger study in oils. She worked upon it in her own room every moment she could spare from her studio practice, unknown to her professor. It absorbed her existence; she grew thin and pale. When it was finished, and only then, she showed it tremblingly to her master. He stood silent, in profound astonishment. The easel before him showed a foreground of tangled luxuriance, from which stretched a sheet of water like a darkened mirror, while through parted reeds on its glossy surface arose the half-submerged figure of a river god, exquisite in contour, yet whose delicate outlines were almost a vision by the crowning illusion of light, shadow, and atmosphere.

"It is a beautiful copy, mademoiselle, and I forgive you breaking my rules," he said, drawing a long breath. "But I cannot now recall the original picture."

"It's no copy of a picture, professor," said the young girl timidly, and she disclosed her secret. "It was the only perfect statue there," she added diffidently; "but I think it wanted—something."

"True," said the professor abstractedly. "Where the elbow rests there should be a half-inverted urn flowing with water; but the drawing of that shoulder is so perfect—as is YOUR study of it—that one guesses the missing forearm one cannot see, which clasped it. Beautiful! beautiful!"

Suddenly he stopped, and turned his eyes almost searchingly on hers.

"You say you have never drawn from the human model, mademoiselle?"

"Never," said the young girl innocently.

"True," murmured the professor again. "These are the classic ideal measurements. There are no limbs like those now. Yet it is wonderful! And this gem, you say, is in England?"

"Yes."

"Good! I am going there in a few days. I shall make a pilgrimage to see it. Until then, mademoiselle, I beg you to break as many of my rules as you like."

Three weeks later she found the professor one morning standing before her picture in her private studio. "You have returned from England," she said joyfully.

"I have," said the professor gravely.

"You have seen the original subject?" she said timidly.

"I have NOT. I have not seen it, mademoiselle," he said, gazing at her mildly through his glasses, "because it does not exist, and never existed."

The young girl turned pale.

"Listen. I have go to England. I arrive at the Park of Domesday. I penetrate the beautiful, wild garden. I approach the fountain. I see the wonderful water, the exquisite light and shade, the lilies, the mysterious reeds—beautiful, yet not as beautiful as you have made it, mademoiselle, but no statue—no river god! I demand it of the concierge. He knows of it absolutely nothing. I transport myself to the noble proprietor, Monsieur le Duc, at a distant chateau where he has collected the ruined marbles. It is not there."

"Yet I saw it," said the young girl earnestly, yet with a troubled face. "O professor," she burst out appealingly, "what do you think it was?"

"I think, mademoiselle," said the professor gravely, "that you created it. Believe me, it is a function of genius! More, it is a proof, a necessity! You saw the beautiful lake, the ruined fountain, the soft shadows, the empty plinth, curtained by reeds. You yourself say you feel there was 'something wanting.' Unconsciously you yourself supplied it. All that you had ever dreamt of mythology, all that you had ever seen of statuary, thronged upon you at that supreme moment, and, evolved from your own fancy, the river god was born. It is your own, chere enfant, as much the offspring of your genius as the exquisite atmosphere you have caught, the charm of light and shadow that you have brought away. Accept my felicitations. You have little more to learn of me."

As he bowed himself out and descended the stairs he shrugged his shoulders slightly. "She is an adorable genius," he murmured. "Yet she is also a woman. Being a woman, naturally she has a lover—this river god! Why not?"

The extraordinary success of Miss Forrest's picture and the instantaneous recognition of her merit as an artist, apart from her novel subject, perhaps went further to remove her uneasiness than any serious conviction of the professor's theory. Nevertheless, it appealed to her poetic and mystic imagination, and although other subjects from her brush met with equally phenomenal success, and she was able in a year to return to America with a reputation assured beyond criticism, she never entirely forgot the strange incident connected with her initial effort.

And by degrees a singular change came over her. Rich, famous, and attractive, she began to experience a sentimental and romantic interest in that episode. Once, when reproached by her friends for her indifference to her admirers, she had half laughingly replied that she had once found her "ideal," but never would again. Yet the jest had scarcely passed her lips before she became pale and silent. With this change came also a desire to re-purchase the picture, which she had sold in her early success to a speculative American picture-dealer. On inquiry she found, alas! that it had been sold only a day or two before to a Chicago gentleman, of the name of Potter, who had taken a fancy to it.

Miss Forrest curled her pretty lip, but, nothing daunted, resolved to effect her purpose, and sought the purchaser at his hotel. She was ushered into a private drawing-room, where, on a handsome easel, stood the newly acquired purchase. Mr. Potter was out, "but would return in a moment."

Miss Forrest was relieved, for, alone and undisturbed, she could now let her full soul go out to her romantic creation. As she stood there, she felt the glamour of the old English garden come back to her, the play of light and shadow, the silent pool, the godlike face and bust, with its cast-down, meditative eyes, seen through the parted reeds. She clasped her hands silently before her. Should she never see it again as then?

"Pray don't let me disturb you; but won't you take a seat?"

Miss Forrest turned sharply round. Then she started, uttered a frightened little cry, and fainted away.

Mr. Potter was touched, but a master of himself. As she came to, he said quietly: "I came upon you suddenly—as you stood entranced by this picture—just as I did when I first saw it. That's why I bought it. Are you any relative of the Miss Forrest who painted it?" he continued, quietly looking at her card, which he held in his hand.

Miss Forrest recovered herself sufficiently to reply, and stated her business with some dignity.

"Ah," said Mr. Potter, "THAT is another question. You see, the picture has a special value to me, as I once saw an old-fashioned garden like that in England. But that chap there,— I beg your pardon, I mean that figure,—I fancy, is your own creation, entirely. However, I'll think over your proposition, and if you will allow me I'll call and see you about it."

Mr. Potter did call—not once, but many times—and showed quite a remarkable interest in Miss Forrest's art. The question of the sale of the picture, however, remained in abeyance. A few weeks later, after a longer call than usual, Mr. Potter said:—

"Don't you think the best thing we can do is to make a kind of compromise, and let us own the picture together?"

And they did.

A ROMANCE OF THE LINE

As the train moved slowly out of the station, the Writer of Stories looked up wearily from the illustrated pages of the magazines and weeklies on his lap to the illustrated advertisements on the walls of the station sliding past his carriage windows. It was getting to be monotonous. For a while he had been hopefully interested in the bustle of the departing trains, and looked up from his comfortable and early invested position to the later comers with that sense of superiority common to travelers; had watched the conventional leave-takings—always feebly prolonged to the uneasiness of both parties—and contrasted it with the impassive business promptitude of the railway officials; but it was the old experience repeated. Falling back on the illustrated advertisements again, he wondered if their perpetual recurrence at every station would not at last bring to the tired traveler the loathing of satiety; whether the passenger in railway carriages, continually offered Somebody's oats, inks, washing blue, candles, and soap, apparently as a necessary equipment for a few hours' journey, would not there and thereafter forever ignore the use of these articles, or recoil from that particular quality. Or, as an unbiased observer, he wondered if, on the other hand, impressible passengers, after passing three or four stations, had ever leaped from the train and refused to proceed further until they were supplied with one or more of those articles.

Bret Harte

Had he ever known any one who confided to him in a moment of expansiveness that he had dated his use of Somebody's soap to an advertisement persistently borne upon him through the medium of a railway carriage window? No! Would he not have connected that man with that other certifying individual who always appends a name and address singularly obscure and unconvincing, yet who, at some supreme moment, recommends Somebody's pills to a dying friend,—afflicted with a similar address,—which restore him to life and undying obscurity. Yet these pictorial and literary appeals must have a potency independent of the wares they advertise, or they wouldn't be there.

Perhaps he was the more sensitive to this monotony as he was just then seeking change and novelty in order to write a new story. He was not looking for material,—his subjects were usually the same,—he was merely hoping for that relaxation and diversion which should freshen and fit him for later concentration. Still, he had often heard of the odd circumstances to which his craft were sometimes indebted for suggestion. The invasion of an eccentric-looking individual—probably an innocent tradesman into a railway carriage had given the hint for "A Night with a Lunatic;" a nervously excited and belated passenger had once unconsciously sat for an escaped forger; the picking up of a forgotten novel in the rack, with passages marked in pencil, had afforded the plot of a love story; or the germ of a romance had been found in an obscure news paragraph which, under less listless moments, would have passed unread. On the other hand, he recalled these inconvenient and inconsistent moments from which the so-called "inspiration" sprang, the utter incongruity of time and place in some brilliant conception, and wondered if sheer vacuity of mind were really so favorable.

Going back to his magazine again, he began to get mildly

interested in a story. Turning the page, however, he was confronted by a pictorial advertising leaflet inserted between the pages, yet so artistic in character that it might have been easily mistaken for an illustration of the story he was reading, and perhaps was not more remote or obscure in reference than many he had known. But the next moment he recognized with despair that it was only a smaller copy of one he had seen on the hoarding at the last station. He threw the leaflet aside, but the flavor of the story was gone. The peerless detergent of the advertisement had erased it from the tablets of his memory. He leaned back in his seat again, and lazily watched the flying suburbs. Here were the usual promising open spaces and patches of green, quickly succeeded again by solid blocks of houses whose rear windows gave directly upon the line, yet seldom showed an inquisitive face—even of a wondering child. It was a strange revelation of the depressing effects of familiarity. Expresses might thunder by, goods trains drag their slow length along, shunting trains pipe all day beneath their windows, but the tenants heeded them not. Here, too, was the junction, with its labyrinthine interlacing of tracks that dazed the tired brain; the overburdened telegraph posts, that looked as if they really could not stand another wire; the long lines of empty, homeless, and deserted trains in sidings that had seen better days; the idle trains, with staring vacant windows, which were eventually seized by a pert engine hissing, "Come along, will you?" and departed with a discontented grunt from every individual carriage coupling; the racing trains, that suddenly appeared parallel with one's carriage windows, begot false hopes of a challenge of speed, and then, without warning, drew contemptuously and, superciliously away; the swift eclipse of everything in a tunneled bridge; the long, slithering passage of an "up" express, and then the flash of a station, incoherent and unintelligible with pictorial advertisements again.

He closed his eyes to concentrate his thought, and by degrees a pleasant languor stole over him. The train had by this time attained that rate of speed which gave it a slight swing and roll on curves and switches not unlike the rocking of a cradle. Once or twice he opened his eyes sleepily upon the waltzing trees in the double planes of distance, and again closed them. Then, in one of these slight oscillations, he felt himself ridiculously slipping into slumber, and awoke with some indignation. Another station was passed, in which process the pictorial advertisements on the hoardings and the pictures in his lap seemed to have become jumbled up, confused, and to dance before him, and then suddenly and strangely, without warning, the train stopped short—at ANOTHER station. And then he arose, and—what five minutes before he never conceived of doing—gathered his papers and slipped from the carriage to the platform. When I say "he" I mean, of course, the Writer of Stories; yet the man who slipped out was half his age and a different-looking person.

*****

The change from the motion of the train—for it seemed that he had been traveling several hours—to the firmer platform for a moment bewildered him. The station looked strange, and he fancied it lacked a certain kind of distinctness. But that quality was also noticeable in the porters and loungers on the platform. He thought it singular, until it seemed to him that they were not characteristic, nor in any way important or necessary to the business he had in hand. Then, with an effort, he tried to remember himself and his purpose, and made his way through the station to the open road beyond. A van, bearing the inscription, "Removals to Town and Country," stood before him and blocked his way, but a dogcart was in waiting, and a grizzled groom, who held the reins, touched his hat respectfully. Although still dazed by his journey and uncertain of himself, he seemed to recognize in the man that distinctive character which was wanting in the others. The correctness of his surmise was revealed a few moments later, when, after he had taken his seat beside him, and they were rattling out of the village street, the man turned towards him and said:—

"Tha'll know Sir Jarge?"

"I do not," said the young man.

"Ay! but theer's many as cooms here as doan't, for all they cooms. Tha'll say it ill becooms mea as war man and boy in Sir Jarge's sarvice for fifty year, to say owt agen him, but I'm here to do it, or they couldn't foolfil their business. Tha wast to ax me questions about Sir Jarge and the Grange, and I wor to answer soa as to make tha think thar was suthing wrong wi' un. Howbut I may save tha time and tell thea downroight that Sir Jarge forged his uncle's will, and so gotten the Grange. That 'ee keeps his niece in mortal fear o' he. That tha'll be put in haunted chamber wi' a boggle."

"I think," said the young man hesitatingly, "that there must be some mistake. I do not know any Sir George, and I am NOT going to the Grange."

"Eay! Then thee aren't the 'ero sent down from London by the story writer?"

"Not by THAT one," said the young man diffidently.

The old man's face changed. It was no mere figure of speech: it actually was ANOTHER face that looked down upon the traveler.

"Then mayhap your honor will be bespoken at the Angel's Inn," he said, with an entirely distinct and older dialect, "and a finer hostel for a young gentleman of your condition ye'll not find on this side of Oxford. A fair chamber, looking to the sun; sheets smelling of lavender from Dame Margery's own store, and, for the matter of that, spread by the fair hands of Maudlin, her daughter—the best favored lass that ever danced under a Maypole. Ha! have at ye there, young sir! Not to speak of the October ale of old Gregory, her father—ay, nor the rare Hollands, that never paid excise duties to the king."

"I'm afraid," said the young traveler timidly, "there's over a century between us. There's really some mistake."

"What?" said the groom, "ye are NOT the young spark who is to marry Mistress Amy at the Hall, yet makes a pother and mess of it all by a duel with Sir Roger de Cadgerly, the wicked baronet, for his over-free discourse with our fair Maudlin this very eve? Ye are NOT the traveler whose post-chaise is now at the Falcon? Ye are not he that was bespoken by the story writer in London?"

"I don't think I am," said the young man apologetically. "Indeed, as I am feeling far from well, I think I'll get out and walk."

He got down—the vehicle and driver vanished in the distance. It did not surprise him. "I must collect my thoughts," he said. He did so. Possibly the collection was not large, for presently he said, with a sigh of relief:—

"I see it all now! My name is Paul Bunker. I am of the young branch of an old Quaker family, rich and respected in the country, and I am on a visit to my ancestral home. But I have lived since a child in America, and am alien to the traditions and customs of the old country, and even of the seat to which my fathers belong. I have brought with me from the far West many peculiarities of speech and thought that may startle my kinsfolk. But I certainly shall not address my uncle as 'Hoss!' nor shall I say 'guess' oftener than is necessary."

Much brightened and refreshed by his settled identity, he had time, as he walked briskly along, to notice the scenery, which was certainly varied and conflicting in character, and quite inconsistent with his preconceived notions of an English landscape. On his right, a lake of the brightest cobalt blue stretched before a many-towered and terraced town, which was relieved by a background of luxuriant foliage and emerald-green mountains; on his left arose a rugged mountain, which he was surprised to see was snow-capped, albeit a tunnel was observable midway of its height, and a train just issuing from it. Almost regretting that he had not continued on his journey, as he was fully sensible that it was in some way connected with the railway he had quitted, presently his attention was directed to the gateway of a handsome park, whose mansion was faintly seen in the distance. Hurrying towards him, down the avenue of limes, was a strange figure. It was that of a man of middle age; clad in Quaker garb, yet with an extravagance of cut and detail which seemed antiquated even for England. He had evidently seen the young man approaching, and his face was beaming with welcome. If Paul had doubted that it was his uncle, the first words he spoke would have reassured him.

"Welcome to Hawthorn Hall," said the figure, grasping his hand heartily, "but thee will excuse me if I do not tarry with thee long at present, for I am hastening, even now, with some nourishing and sustaining food for Giles Hayward, a farm laborer." He pointed to a package he was carrying. "But thee will find thy cousins Jane and Dorcas Bunker taking tea in the summer-house. Go to them! Nay—positively—I may not linger, but will return to thee quickly." And, to Paul's astonishment, he trotted away on his sturdy, respectable legs, still beaming and carrying his package in his hand.

"Well, I'll be dog-goned! but the old man ain't going to be left, you bet!" he ejaculated, suddenly remembering his dialect. "He'll get there, whether school keeps or not!" Then, reflecting that no one heard him, he added simply, "He certainly was not over civil towards the nephew he has never seen before. And those girls—whom I don't know! How very awkward!"

Nevertheless, he continued his way up the avenue towards the mansion. The park was beautifully kept. Remembering the native wildness and virgin seclusion of the Western forest, he could not help contrasting it with the conservative gardening of this pretty woodland, every rood of which had been patrolled by keepers and rangers, and preserved and fostered hundreds of years before he was born, until warmed for human occupancy. At times the avenue was crossed by grass drives, where the original woodland had been displaced, not by the exigency of a "clearing" for tillage, as in his own West, but for the leisurely pleasure of the owner. Then, a few hundred yards from the house itself,—a quaint Jacobean mansion,—he came to an open space where the sylvan landscape had yielded to floral cultivation, and so fell upon a charming summer-house, or arbor, embowered with roses. It must have been the one of which his uncle had spoken, for there, to his wondering admiration, sat two little maids before a rustic table, drinking tea demurely, yes, with all the evident delight of a childish escapade from their elders. While in the picturesque quaintness of their attire there was still a formal suggestion of the sect to which their father belonged, their summer frocks—differing in color, yet each of the same subdued tint—were alike in cut and fashion, and short enough to show their dainty feet in prim slippers and silken hose that matched their frocks. As the afternoon sun glanced through the leaves upon their pink cheeks, tied up in quaint hats by ribbons under their chins, they made a charming picture. At least Paul thought so as he advanced towards them, hat in hand. They looked up at his approach, but again cast down their eyes with demure shyness; yet he fancied that they first exchanged glances with each other, full of mischievous intelligence.

"I am your cousin Paul," he said smilingly, "though I am afraid I am introducing myself almost as briefly as your father just now excused himself to me. He told me I would find you here, but he himself was hastening on a Samaritan mission."

"With a box in his hand?" said the girls simultaneously, exchanging glances with each other again.

"With a box containing some restorative, I think," responded Paul, a little wonderingly.

"Restorative! So THAT'S what he calls it now, is it?" said one of the girls saucily. "Well, no one knows what's in the box, though he always carries it with him. Thee never sees him without it"—

"And a roll of paper," suggested the other girl.

"Yes, a roll of paper—but one never knows what it is!" said the first speaker. "It's very strange. But no matter now, Paul. Welcome to Hawthorn Hall. I am Jane Bunker, and this is Dorcas." She stopped, and then, looking down demurely, added, "Thee may kiss us both, cousin Paul."

The young man did not wait for a second invitation, but gently touched his lips to their soft young cheeks.

"Thee does not speak like an American, Paul. Is thee really

and truly one?" continued Jane.

Paul remembered that he had forgotten his dialect, but it was too late now.

"I am really and truly one, and your own cousin, and I hope you will find me a very dear"—

"Oh!" said Dorcas, starting up primly. "You must really allow me to withdraw." To the young man's astonishment, she seized her parasol, and, with a youthful affectation of dignity, glided from the summer-house and was lost among the trees.

"Thy declaration to me was rather sudden," said Jane quietly, in answer to his look of surprise, "and Dorcas is peculiarly sensitive and less like the 'world's people' than I am. And it was just a little cruel, considering that she has loved thee secretly all these years, followed thy fortunes in America with breathless eagerness, thrilled at thy narrow escapes, and wept at thy privations."

"But she has never seen me before!" said the astounded Paul.

"And thee had never seen me before, and yet thee has dared to propose to me five minutes after thee arrived, and in her presence."

"But, my dear girl!" expostulated Paul.

"Stand off!" she said, rapidly opening her parasol and interposing it between them. "Another step nearer—ay, even another word of endearment—and I shall be compelled— nay, forced," she added in a lower voice, "to remove this parasol, lest it should be crushed and ruined!"

"I see," he said gloomily, "you have been reading novels; but so have I, and the same ones! Nevertheless, I intended only to tell you that I hoped you would always find me a kind friend."

She shut her parasol up with a snap. "And I only intended to tell thee that my heart was given to another."

"You INTENDED—and now?"

"Is it the 'kind friend' who asks?"

"If it were not?"

"Really?"

"Yes."

"Ah!"

"Oh!"

"But thee loves another?" she said, toying with her cup.

He attempted to toy with his, but broke it. A man lacks delicacy in this kind of persiflage. "You mean I am loved by another," he said bluntly.

"You dare to say that!" she said, flashing, in spite of her prim demeanor.

"No, but YOU did just now! You said your sister loved me!"

"Did I?" she said dreamily. "Dear! dear! That's the trouble of trying to talk like Mr. Blank's delightful dialogues. One gets so mixed!"

"Yet you will be a sister to me?" he said. "'Tis an old American joke, but 'twill serve."

There was a long silence.

"Had thee not better go to sister Dorcas? She is playing with the cows," said Jane plaintively.

"You forget," he returned gravely, "that, on page 27 of the novel we have both read, at this point he is supposed to kiss her."

She had forgotten, but they both remembered in time. At this moment a scream came faintly from the distance. They both started, and rose.

"It is sister Dorcas," said Jane, sitting down again and pouring out another cup of tea. "I have always told her that one of those Swiss cows would hook her."

Paul stared at her with a strange revulsion of feeling. "I could save Dorcas," he muttered to himself, "in less time than it takes to describe." He paused, however, as he reflected that this would depend entirely upon the methods of the writer of this description. "I could rescue her! I have only to take the first clothes-line that I find, and with that knowledge and skill with the lasso which I learned in the wilds of America, I could stop the charge of the most furious ruminant. I will!" and without another word he turned and rushed off in the direction of the sound.

*****

He had not gone a hundred yards before he paused, a little bewildered. To the left could still be seen the cobalt lake with the terraced background; to the right the rugged mountains. He chose the latter. Luckily for him a cottager's garden lay in his path, and from a line supported by a single pole depended the homely linen of the cottager. To tear these garments from the line was the work of a moment (although it represented the whole week's washing), and hastily coiling the rope dexterously in his hand, he sped onward. Already panting with exertion and excitement, a few roods farther he was confronted with a spectacle that left him breathless.

A woman—young, robust, yet gracefully formed—was running ahead of him, driving before her with an open parasol an animal which he instantly recognized as one of that simple yet treacherous species most feared by the sex—known as the "Moo Cow."

For a moment he was appalled by the spectacle. But it was only for a moment! Recalling his manhood and her weakness, he stopped, and bracing his foot against a stone, with a graceful flourish of his lasso around his head, threw it in the air. It uncoiled slowly, sped forward with unerring precision, and missed! With the single cry of "Saved!" the fair stranger sank fainting in his arms! He held her closely until the color came back to her pale face. Then he quietly disentangled the lasso from his legs.

"Where am I?" she said faintly.

"In the same place," he replied, slowly but firmly. "But," he added, "you have changed!"

She had, indeed, even to her dress. It was now of a vivid brick red, and so much longer in the skirt that it seemed to make her taller. Only her hat remained the same.

"Yes," she said, in a low, reflective voice and a disregard of her previous dialect, as she gazed up in his eyes with an eloquent lucidity, "I have changed, Paul! I feel myself changing at those words you uttered to Jane. There are moments in a woman's life that man knows nothing of; moments bitter and cruel, sweet and merciful, that change her whole being; moments in which the simple girl becomes a worldly woman; moments in which the slow procession of her years is never noted—except by another woman! Moments that change her outlook on the world and her relations to it—and her husband's relations! Moments when the maid becomes a wife, the wife a widow, the widow a re-married woman, by a simple, swift illumination of the fancy. Moments when, wrought upon by a single word—a look—an emphasis and rising inflection, all logical sequence is cast away, processes are lost—inductions lead nowhere. Moments when the inharmonious becomes harmonious, the indiscreet discreet, the inefficient efficient, and the inevitable evitable. I mean," she corrected herself hurriedly—"You know what I mean! If you have not felt it you have read it!"

"I have," he said thoughtfully. "We have both read it in the same novel. She is a fine writer."

"Ye-e-s." She hesitated with that slight resentment of praise of another woman so delightful in her sex. "But you have forgotten the Moo Cow!" and she pointed to where the distracted animal was careering across the lawn towards the garden.

"You are right," he said, "the incident is not yet closed. Let us pursue it."

They both pursued it. Discarding the useless lasso, he had recourse to a few well-aimed epithets. The infuriated animal swerved and made directly towards a small fountain in the centre of the garden. In attempting to clear it, it fell directly into the deep cup-like basin and remained helplessly fixed, with its fore-legs projecting uneasily beyond the rim.

"Let us leave it there," she said, "and forget it—and all that has gone before. Believe me," she added, with a faint sigh, "it is best. Our paths diverge from this moment. I go to the summer-house, and you go to the Hall, where my father is expecting you." He would have detained her a moment longer, but she glided away and was gone.

Left to himself again, that slight sense of bewilderment which had clouded his mind for the last hour began to clear away; his singular encounter with the girls strangely enough affected him less strongly than his brief and unsatisfactory interview with his uncle. For, after all, he was his host, and upon him depended his stay at Hawthorn Hall. The mysterious and slighting allusions of his cousins to the old man's eccentricities also piqued his curiosity. Why had they sneered at his description of the contents of the package he carried—and what did it really contain? He did not reflect that it was none of his business,—people in his situation seldom do,—and he eagerly hurried towards the Hall. But he found in his preoccupation he had taken the wrong turning in the path, and that he was now close to the wall which bounded and overlooked the highway. Here a singular spectacle presented itself. A cyclist covered with dust was seated in the middle of the road, trying to restore circulation to his bruised and injured leg by chafing it with his hands, while beside him lay his damaged bicycle. He had evidently met with an accident. In an instant Paul had climbed the wall and was at his side.

"Can I offer you any assistance?" he asked eagerly.

"Thanks—no! I've come a beastly cropper over something or other on this road, and I'm only bruised, though the machine has suffered worse," replied the stranger, in a fresh, cheery voice. He was a good-looking fellow of about Paul's own age, and the young American's heart went out towards him.

"How did it happen?" asked Paul.

"That's what puzzles me," said the stranger. "I was getting out of the way of a queer old chap in the road, and I ran over something that seemed only an old scroll of paper; but the shock was so great that I was thrown, and I fancy I was for a few moments unconscious. Yet I cannot see any other obstruction in the road, and there's only that bit of paper." He pointed to the paper,—a half-crushed roll of ordinary foolscap, showing the mark of the bicycle upon it.

A strange idea came into Paul's mind. He picked up the paper and examined it closely. Besides the mark already indicated, it showed two sharp creases about nine inches long, and another exactly at the point of the impact of the bicycle. Taking a folded two-foot rule from his pocket, he carefully measured these parallel creases and made an exhaustive geometrical calculation with his pencil on the paper. The stranger watched him with awed and admiring interest. Rising, he again carefully examined the road, and was finally rewarded by the discovery of a sharp indentation in the dust, which, on measurement and comparison with the creases in the paper and the calculations he had just made, proved to be identical.

"There was a solid body in that paper," said Paul quietly; "a parallelogram exactly nine inches long and three wide."

"I say! you're wonderfully clever, don't you know," said the stranger, with unaffected wonder. "I see it all—a brick."

Paul smiled gently and shook his head. "That is the hasty inference of an inexperienced observer. You will observe at the point of impact of your wheel the parallel crease is CURVED, as from the yielding of the resisting substances, and not BROKEN, as it would be by the crumbling of a brick."

"I say, you're awfully detective, don't you know! just like that fellow—what's his name?" said the stranger admiringly.

The words recalled Paul to himself. Why was he acting like a detective? and what was he seeking to discover? Nevertheless, he felt impelled to continue. "And that queer old chap whom you met—why didn't he help you?"

"Because I passed him before I ran into the—the parallelogram, and I suppose he didn't know what happened behind him?"

"Did he have anything in his hand?"

"Can't say."

"And you say you were unconscious afterwards?"

"Yes!"

"Long enough for the culprit to remove the principal evidence of his crime?"

"Come! I say, really you are—you know you are!"

"Have you any secret enemy?"

"No."

"And you don't know Mr. Bunker, the man who owns this vast estate?"

"Not at all. I'm from Upper Tooting."

"Good afternoon," said Paul abruptly, and turned away.

It struck him afterwards that his action might have seemed uncivil, and even inhuman, to the bruised cyclist, who could hardly walk. But it was getting late, and he was still far from the Hall, which, oddly enough, seemed to be no longer visible from the road. He wandered on for some time, half convinced that he had passed the lodge gates, yet hoping to find some other entrance to the domain. Dusk was falling; the rounded outlines of the park trees beyond the wall were solid masses of shadow. The full moon, presently rising, restored them again to symmetry, and at last he, to his relief, came upon the massive gateway. Two lions ramped in stone on the side pillars. He thought it strange that he had not noticed the gateway on his previous entrance, but he remembered that he was fully preoccupied with the advancing figure of his uncle. In a few minutes the Hall itself appeared, and here again he was surprised that he had overlooked before its noble proportions and picturesque outline. Its broad terraces, dazzlingly white in the moonlight; its long line of mullioned windows, suffused with a warm red glow from within, made it look like part of a wintry landscape—and suggested a Christmas card. The venerable ivy that hid the ravages time had made in its walls looked like black carving. His heart swelled with strange emotions as he gazed at his ancestral hall. How many of his blood had lived and died there; how many had gone forth from that great porch to distant lands! He tried to think of his father—a little child—peeping between the balustrades of that terrace. He tried to think of it, and perhaps would have succeeded had it not occurred to him that it was a known fact that his uncle had bought the estate and house of an impoverished nobleman only the year before. Yet—he could not tell why—he seemed to feel higher and nobler for that trial.

The terrace was deserted, and so quiet that as he ascended to it his footsteps seemed to echo from the walls. When he reached the portals, the great oaken door swung noiselessly on its hinges—opened by some unseen but waiting servitor—and admitted him to a lofty hall, dark with hangings and family portraits, but warmed by a red carpet the whole length of its stone floor. For a moment he waited for the servant to show him to the drawing-room or his uncle's study. But no one appeared. Believing this to be a part of the characteristic simplicity of the Quaker household, he boldly entered the first door, and found himself in a brilliantly lit and perfectly empty drawing-room. The same experience met him with the other rooms on that floor—the dining-room displaying an already set, exquisitely furnished and decorated table, with chairs for twenty guests! He mechanically ascended the wide oaken staircase that led to the corridor of bedrooms above a central salon. Here he found only the same solitude. Bedroom doors yielded to his touch, only to show the same brilliantly lit vacancy. He presently came upon one room which seemed to give unmistakable signs of HIS OWN occupancy. Surely there stood his own dressing-case on the table! and his own evening clothes carefully laid out on another, as if fresh from a valet's hands. He stepped hastily into the corridor—there was no one there; he rang the bell—there was no response! But he noticed that there was a jug of hot water in his basin, and he began dressing mechanically.

There was little doubt that he was in a haunted house, but this did not particularly disturb him. Indeed, he found himself wondering if it could be logically called a haunted house—unless he himself was haunting it, for there seemed to be no other there. Perhaps the apparitions would come later, when he was dressed. Clearly it was not his uncle's house—and yet, as he had never been inside his uncle's house, he reflected that he ought not to be positive.

He finished dressing and sat down in an armchair with a kind of thoughtful expectancy. But presently his curiosity became impatient of the silence and mystery, and he ventured once more to explore the house. Opening his bedroom door, he found himself again upon the deserted corridor, but this time he could distinctly hear a buzz of voices from the drawing-room below. Assured that he was near a solution of the mystery, he rapidly descended the broad staircase and made his way to the open door of the drawing-room. But although the sound of voices increased as he advanced, when he entered the room, to his utter astonishment, it was as empty as before.

Yet, in spite of his bewilderment and confusion, he was able to follow one of the voices, which, in its peculiar distinctness and half-perfunctory tone, he concluded must belong to the host of the invisible assembly.

"Ah," said the voice, greeting some unseen visitor, "so glad you have come. Afraid your engagements just now would keep you away." Then the voice dropped to a lower and more confidential tone. "You must take down Lady Dartman, but you will have Miss Morecamp—a clever girl—on the other side of you. Ah, Sir George! So good of you to come. All well at the Priory? So glad to hear it." (Lower and more confidentially.) "You know Mrs. Monkston. You'll sit by her. A little cut up by her husband losing his seat. Try to amuse her."

Emboldened by desperation, Paul turned in the direction of the voice. "I am Paul Bunker," he said hesitatingly. "I'm afraid you'll think me intrusive, but I was looking for my uncle, and"—

"Intrusive, my dear boy! The son of my near neighbor in the country intrusive? Really, now, I like that! Grace!" (the voice turned in another direction) "here is the American nephew of our neighbor Bunker at Widdlestone, who thinks he is 'a stranger.'"

"We all knew of your expected arrival at Widdlestone—it was so good of you to waive ceremony and join us," said a well-bred feminine voice, which Paul at once assumed to belong to the hostess. "But I must find some one for your dinner partner. Mary" (here her voice was likewise turned away), "this is Mr. Bunker, the nephew of an old friend and neighbor in Upshire;" (the voice again turned to him), "you will take Miss Morecamp in. My dear" (once again averted), "I must find some one else to console poor dear Lord Billingtree with." Here the hostess's voice was drowned by fresh arrivals.

Bewildered and confused as he was, standing in this empty desert of a drawing-room, yet encompassed on every side by human voices, so marvelous was the power of suggestion, he seemed to almost feel the impact of the invisible crowd. He was trying desperately to realize his situation when a singularly fascinating voice at his elbow unexpectedly assisted him. It was evidently his dinner partner.

"I suppose you must be tired after your journey. When did you arrive?"

"Only a few hours ago," said Paul.

"And I dare say you haven't slept since you arrived. One doesn't on the passage, you know; the twenty hours pass so quickly, and the experience is so exciting—to US at least. But I suppose as an American you are used to it."

Paul gasped. He had passively accepted the bodiless conversation, because it was at least intelligible! But NOW! Was he going mad?

She evidently noticed his silence. "Never mind," she continued, "you can tell me all about it at dinner. Do you know I always think that this sort of thing—what we're doing now,—this ridiculous formality of reception,—which I suppose is after all only a concession to our English force of habit,—is absurd! We ought to pass, as it were, directly from our houses to the dinner-table. It saves time."

"Yes—no—that is—I'm afraid I don't follow you," stammered Paul.

There was a slight pout in her voice as she replied: "No matter now—we must follow them—for our host is moving off with Lady Billingtree, and it's our turn now."

So great was the illusion that he found himself mechanically offering his arm as he moved through the empty room towards the door. Then he descended the staircase without another word, preceded, however, by the sound of his host's voice. Following this as a blind man might, he entered the dining-room, which to his discomfiture was as empty as the salon above. Still following the host's voice, he dropped into a chair before the empty table, wondering what variation of the Barmecide feast was in store for him. Yet the hum of voices from the vacant chairs around the board so strongly impressed him that he could almost believe that he was actually at dinner.

"Are you seated?" asked the charming voice at his side.

"Yes," a little wonderingly, as his was the only seat visibly occupied.

"I am so glad that this silly ceremony is over. By the way, where are you?"

Paul would have liked to answer, "Lord only knows!" but he reflected that it might not sound polite. "Where am I?" he feebly repeated.

"Yes; where are you dining?"

It seemed a cool question under the circumstances, but he answered promptly,—

"With you."

"Of course," said the charming voice; "but where are you eating your dinner?"

Considering that he was not eating anything, Paul thought this cooler still. But he answered briefly, "In Upshire."

"Oh! At your uncle's?"

"No," said Paul bluntly; "in the next house."

"Why, that's Sir William's—our host's—and he and his family are here in London. You are joking."

"Listen!" said Paul desperately. Then in a voice unconsciously lowered he hurriedly told her where he was—how he came there—the empty house—the viewless company! To his surprise the only response was a musical little laugh. But the next moment her voice rose higher with an unmistakable concern in it, apparently addressing their invisible host.

"Oh, Sir William, only think how dreadful. Here's poor Mr. Bunker, alone in an empty house, which he has mistaken for his uncle's—and without any dinner!"

"Really; dear, dear! How provoking! But how does he

happen to be WITH US? James, how is this?"

"If you please, Sir William," said a servant's respectful voice, "Widdlestone is in the circuit and is switched on with the others. We heard that a gentleman's luggage had arrived at Widdlestone, and we telegraphed for the rooms to be made ready, thinking we'd have her ladyship's orders later."

A single gleam of intelligence flashed upon Paul. His luggage—yes, had been sent from the station to the wrong house, and he had unwittingly followed. But these voices! whence did they come? And where was the actual dinner at which his host was presiding? It clearly was not at this empty table.

"See that he has everything he wants at once," said Sir William; "there must be some one there." Then his voice turned in the direction of Paul again, and he said laughingly, "Possess your soul and appetite in patience for a moment, Mr. Bunker; you will be only a course behind us. But we are lucky in having your company—even at your own discomfort."

Still more bewildered, Paul turned to his invisible partner. "May I ask where YOU are dining?"

"Certainly; at home in Curzon Street," returned the pretty voice. "It was raining so, I did not go out."

"And—Lord Billington?" faltered Paul.

"Oh, he's in Scotland—at his own place."

"Then, in fact, nobody is dining here at all," said Paul desperately.

There was a slight pause, and then the voice responded, with a touch of startled suggestion in it: "Good heavens, Mr. Bunker! Is it possible you don't know we're dining by telephone?"

"By what?"

"Telephone. Yes. We're a telephonic dinner-party. We are dining in our own houses; but, being all friends, we're switched on to each other, and converse exactly as we would at table. It saves a great trouble and expense, for any one of us can give the party, and the poorest can equal the most extravagant. People who are obliged to diet can partake of their own slops at home, and yet mingle with the gourmets without awkwardness or the necessity of apology. We are spared the spectacle, at least, of those who eat and drink too much. We can switch off a bore at once. We can retire when we are fatigued, without leaving a blank space before the others. And all this without saying anything of the higher spiritual and intellectual effect—freed from material grossness of appetite and show—which the dinner party thus attains. But you are surely joking! You, an American, and not know it! Why, it comes from Boston. Haven't you read that book, 'Jumping a Century'? It's by an American."

A strange illumination came upon Paul. Where had he heard something like this before? But at the same moment his thoughts were diverted by the material entrance of a footman, bearing a silver salver with his dinner. It was part of his singular experience that the visible entrance of this real, commonplace mortal—the only one he had seen—in the midst of this voiceless solitude was distinctly unreal, and had all the effect of an apparition. He distrusted it and the dishes before him. But his lively partner's voice was now addressing an unseen occupant of the next chair. Had she got tired of his ignorance, or was it feminine tact to enable him to eat something? He accepted the latter hypothesis, and tried to eat. But he felt himself following the fascinating voice in all the charm of its youthful and spiritual inflections. Taking advantage of its momentary silence, he said gently,—

"I confess my ignorance, and am willing to admit all you claim for this wonderful invention. But do you think it compensates for the loss of the individual person? Take my own case—if you will not think me personal. I have never had the pleasure of seeing you; do you believe that I am content with only that suggestion of your personality which the satisfaction of hearing your voice affords me?"

There was a pause, and then a very mischievous ring in the voice that replied: "It certainly is a personal question, and it is another blessing of this invention that you'll never know whether I am blushing or not; but I forgive you, for I never before spoke to any one I had never seen—and I suppose it's confusion. But do you really think you would know me—the REAL one—any better? It is the real person who thinks and speaks, not the outward semblance that we see, which very often unfairly either attracts or repels us? We can always SHOW ourselves at our best, but we must, at last, reveal our true colors through our thoughts and speech. Isn't it better to begin with the real thing first?"

"I hope, at least, to have the privilege of judging by myself," said Paul gallantly. "You will not be so cruel as not to let me see you elsewhere, otherwise I shall feel as if I were in some dream, and will certainly be opposed to your preference for realities."

"I am not certain if the dream would not be more interesting to you," said the voice laughingly. "But I think your hostess is already saying 'good-by.' You know everybody goes at once at this kind of party; the ladies don't retire first, and the gentlemen join them afterwards. In another moment we'll ALL be switched off; but Sir William wants me to tell you that his coachman will drive you to your uncle's, unless you prefer to try and make yourself comfortable for the night here. Good-by!"

The voices around him seemed to grow fainter, and then utterly cease. The lights suddenly leaped up, went out, and left him in complete darkness. He attempted to rise, but in doing so overset the dishes before him, which slid to the floor. A cold air seemed to blow across his feet. The "good-by" was still ringing in his ears as he straightened himself to find he was in his railway carriage, whose door had just been opened for a young lady who was entering the compartment from a wayside station. "Good-by," she repeated to the friend who was seeing her off. The Writer of Stories hurriedly straightened himself, gathered up the magazines and papers that had fallen from his lap, and glanced at the station walls. The old illustrations glanced back at him! He looked at his watch; he had been asleep just ten minutes!

BOHEMIAN DAYS IN SAN FRANCISCO

It is but just to the respectable memory of San Francisco that in these vagrant recollections I should deprecate at once any suggestion that the levity of my title described its dominant tone at any period of my early experiences. On the contrary, it was a singular fact that while the rest of California was swayed by an easy, careless unconventionalism, or swept over by waves of emotion and sentiment, San Francisco preserved an intensely material and practical attitude, and even a certain austere morality. I do not, of course, allude to the brief days of '49, when it was a straggling beach of huts and stranded hulks, but to the earlier stages of its development into the metropolis of California. Its first tottering steps in that direction were marked by a distinct gravity and decorum. Even during the period when the revolver settled small private difficulties, and Vigilance Committees adjudicated larger public ones, an unmistakable seriousness and respectability was the ruling sign of its governing class. It was not improbable that under the reign of the Committee the lawless and vicious class were more appalled by the moral spectacle of several thousand black-coated, serious-minded business men in embattled procession than by mere force of arms, and one "suspect"—a prize-fighter—is known to have committed suicide in his cell after confrontation with his grave and passionless shop-keeping judges. Even that peculiar quality of Californian humor which was apt to mitigate the extravagances of the revolver and the uncertainties of poker had no place in the decorous and responsible utterance of San Francisco. The press was sober, materialistic, practical—when it was not severely admonitory of existing evil; the few smaller papers that indulged in levity were considered libelous and improper. Fancy was displaced by heavy articles on the revenues of the State and inducements to the investment of capital. Local news was under an implied censorship which suppressed anything that might tend to discourage timid or cautious capital. Episodes of romantic lawlessness or pathetic incidents of mining life were carefully edited—with the comment that these things belonged to the past, and that life and property were now "as safe in San Francisco as in New York or London."

Wonder-loving visitors in quest of scenes characteristic of the civilization were coldly snubbed with this assurance. Fires, floods, and even seismic convulsions were subjected to a like grimly materialistic optimism. I have a vivid recollection of a ponderous editorial on one of the severer earthquakes, in which it was asserted that only the UNEXPECTEDNESS of the onset prevented San Francisco from meeting it in a way that would be deterrent of all future attacks. The unconsciousness of the humor was only equaled by the gravity with which it was received by the whole business community. Strangely enough, this grave materialism flourished side by side with—and was even sustained by—a narrow religious strictness more characteristic of the Pilgrim Fathers of a past century than the Western pioneers of the present. San Francisco was early a city of churches and church organizations to which the leading men and merchants belonged. The lax Sundays of the dying Spanish race seemed only to provoke a revival of the rigors of the Puritan Sabbath. With the Spaniard and his Sunday afternoon bullfight scarcely an hour distant, the San Francisco pulpit thundered against Sunday picnics. One of the popular preachers, declaiming upon the practice of Sunday dinner-giving, averred that when he saw a guest in his best Sunday clothes standing shamelessly upon the doorstep of his host, he felt like seizing him by the shoulder and dragging him from that threshold of perdition.

Against the actual heathen the feeling was even stronger, and reached its climax one Sunday when a Chinaman was stoned to death by a crowd of children returning from Sunday-school. I am offering these examples with no ethical purpose, but merely to indicate a singular contradictory condition which I do not think writers of early Californian history have fairly recorded. It is not my province to suggest any theory for these appalling exceptions to the usual good-humored lawlessness and extravagance of the rest of the State. They may have been essential agencies to the growth and evolution of the city. They were undoubtedly sincere. The impressions I propose to give of certain scenes and incidents of my early experience must, therefore, be taken as purely personal and Bohemian, and their selection as equally individual and vagrant. I am writing of what interested me at the time, though not perhaps of what was more generally characteristic of San Francisco.

I had been there a week—an idle week, spent in listless outlook for employment; a full week in my eager absorption of the strange life around me and a photographic sensitiveness to certain scenes and incidents of those days, which start out of my memory to-day as freshly as the day they impressed me.

One of these recollections is of "steamer night," as it was called,—the night of "steamer day,"—preceding the departure of the mail steamship with the mails for "home." Indeed, at that time San Francisco may be said to have lived from steamer day to steamer day; bills were made due on that day, interest computed to that period, and accounts settled. The next day was the turning of a new leaf: another essay to fortune, another inspiration of energy. So recognized was the fact that even ordinary changes of condition, social and domestic, were put aside until AFTER steamer day. "I'll see what I can do after next steamer day" was the common cautious or hopeful formula. It was the "Saturday night" of many a wage-earner—and to him a night of festivity. The thoroughfares were animated and crowded; the saloons and theatres full. I can recall myself at such times wandering along the City Front, as the business part of San Francisco was then known. Here the lights were burning all night, the first streaks of dawn finding the merchants still at their counting-house desks. I remember the dim lines of warehouses lining the insecure wharves of rotten piles, half filled in—that had ceased to be wharves, but had not yet become streets,—their treacherous yawning depths, with the uncertain gleam of tarlike mud below, at times still vocal with the lap and gurgle of the tide. I remember the weird stories of disappearing men found afterward imbedded in the ooze in which they had fallen and gasped their life away. I remember the two or three ships, still left standing where they were beached a year or two before, built in between warehouses, their bows projecting into the roadway. There was the dignity of the sea and its boundless freedom in their beautiful curves, which the abutting houses could not destroy, and even something of the sea's loneliness in the far-spaced ports and cabin windows lit up by the lamps of the prosaic landsmen who plied their trades behind them. One of these ships, transformed into a hotel, retained its name, the Niantic, and part of its characteristic interior unchanged. I remember these ships' old tenants—the rats—who had increased and multiplied to such an extent that at night they fearlessly crossed the wayfarer's path at every turn, and even invaded the gilded saloons of Montgomery Street. In the Niantic their pit-a-pat was met on every staircase, and it was said that sometimes in an excess of sociability they accompanied the traveler to his room. In the early "cloth-and-papered" houses—so called because the ceilings were not plastered, but simply covered by stretched and white-washed cloth—their scamperings were plainly indicated in zigzag movements of the sagging cloth, or they became actually visible by finally dropping through the holes they had worn in it! I remember the house whose foundations were made of boxes of plug tobacco—part of a jettisoned cargo—used instead of more expensive lumber; and the adjacent warehouse where the trunks of the early and forgotten "forty-niners" were stored, and—never claimed by their dead or missing owners—were finally sold at auction. I remember the strong breath of the sea over all, and the constant onset of the trade winds which helped to disinfect the deposit of dirt and grime, decay and wreckage, which were stirred up in the later evolutions of the city.

Or I recall, with the same sense of youthful satisfaction and unabated wonder, my wanderings through the Spanish Quarter, where three centuries of quaint customs, speech, and dress were still preserved; where the proverbs of Sancho Panza were still spoken in the language of Cervantes, and the high-flown illusions of the La Manchian knight still a part of the Spanish Californian hidalgo's dream. I recall the more modern "Greaser," or Mexican—his index finger steeped in cigarette stains; his velvet jacket and his crimson sash; the many-flounced skirt and lace manta of his women, and their caressing intonations—the one musical utterance of the whole hard-voiced city. I suppose I had a boy's digestion and bluntness of taste in those days, for the combined odor of tobacco, burned paper, and garlic, which marked that melodious breath, did not affect me.

Perhaps from my Puritan training I experienced a more fearful joy in the gambling saloons. They were the largest and most comfortable, even as they were the most expensively decorated rooms in San Francisco. Here again the gravity and decorum which I have already alluded to were present at that earlier period—though perhaps from concentration of another kind. People staked and lost their last dollar with a calm solemnity and a resignation that was almost Christian. The oaths, exclamations, and feverish interruptions which often characterized more dignified assemblies were absent here. There was no room for the lesser vices; there was little or no drunkenness; the gaudily dressed and painted women who presided over the wheels of fortune or performed on the harp and piano attracted no attention from those ascetic players. The man who had won ten thousand dollars and the man who had lost everything rose from the table with equal silence and imperturbability. I never witnessed any tragic sequel to those losses; I never heard of any suicide on account of them. Neither can I recall any quarrel or murder directly attributable to this kind of gambling. It must be remembered that these public games were chiefly rouge et noir, monte, faro, or roulette, in which the antagonist was Fate, Chance, Method, or the impersonal "bank," which was supposed to represent them all; there was no individual opposition or rivalry; nobody challenged the decision of the "croupier," or dealer.

I remember a conversation at the door of one saloon which was as characteristic for its brevity as it was a type of the prevailing stoicism. "Hello!" said a departing miner, as he recognized a brother miner coming in, "when did you come down?" "This morning," was the reply. "Made a strike on the bar?" suggested the first speaker. "You bet!" said the other, and passed in. I chanced an hour later to be at the same place as they met again—their relative positions changed. "Hello! Whar now?" said the incomer. "Back to the bar." "Cleaned out?" "You bet!" Not a word more explained a common situation.

My first youthful experience at those tables was an accidental one. I was watching roulette one evening, intensely absorbed in the mere movement of the players. Either they were so preoccupied with the game, or I was really older looking than my actual years, but a bystander laid his hand familiarly on my shoulder, and said, as to an ordinary habitue, "Ef you're not chippin' in yourself, pardner, s'pose you give ME a show." Now I honestly believe that up to that moment I had no intention, nor even a desire, to try my own fortune. But in the embarrassment of the sudden address I put my hand in my pocket, drew out a coin, and laid it, with an attempt at carelessness, but a vivid consciousness that I was blushing, upon a vacant number. To my horror I saw that I had put down a large coin—the bulk of my possessions! I did not flinch, however; I think any boy who reads this will understand my feeling; it was not only my coin but my manhood at stake. I gazed with a miserable show of indifference at the players, at the chandelier— anywhere but at the dreadful ball spinning round the wheel. There was a pause; the game was declared, the rake rattled up and down, but still I did not look at the table. Indeed, in my inexperience of the game and my embarrassment, I doubt if I should have known if I had won or not. I had made up my mind that I should lose, but I must do so like a man, and, above all, without giving the least suspicion that I was a greenhorn. I even affected to be listening to the music. The wheel spun again; the game was declared, the rake was busy, but I did not move. At last the man I had displaced touched me on the arm and whispered, "Better make a straddle and divide your stake this time." I did not understand him, but as I saw he was looking at the board, I was obliged to look, too. I drew back dazed and bewildered! Where my coin had lain a moment before was a glittering heap of gold.

My stake had doubled, quadrupled, and doubled again. I did not know how much then—I do not know now—it may have been not more than three or four hundred dollars—but it dazzled and frightened me. "Make your game, gentlemen," said the croupier monotonously. I thought he looked at me—indeed, everybody seemed to be looking at me—and my companion repeated his warning. But here I must again appeal to the boyish reader in defense of my idiotic obstinacy. To have taken advice would have shown my youth. I shook my head—I could not trust my voice. I smiled, but with a sinking heart, and let my stake remain. The ball again sped round the wheel, and stopped. There was a pause. The croupier indolently advanced his rake and swept my whole pile with others into the bank! I had lost it all. Perhaps it may be difficult for me to explain why I actually felt relieved, and even to some extent triumphant, but I seemed to have asserted my grown-up independence—possibly at the cost of reducing the number of my meals for days; but what of that! I was a man! I wish I could say that it was a lesson to me. I am afraid it was not. It was true that I did not gamble again, but then I had no especial desire to—and there was no temptation. I am afraid it was an incident without a moral. Yet it had one touch characteristic of the period which I like to remember. The man who had spoken to me, I think, suddenly realized, at the moment of my disastrous coup, the fact of my extreme youth. He moved toward the banker, and leaning over him whispered a few words. The banker looked up, half impatiently, half kindly—his hand straying tentatively toward the pile of coin. I instinctively knew what he meant, and, summoning my determination, met his eyes with all the indifference I could assume, and walked away.

I had at that period a small room at the top of a house owned by a distant relation—a second or third cousin, I think. He was a man of independent and original character, had a Ulyssean experience of men and cities, and an old English name of which he was proud. While in London he had procured from the Heralds' College his family arms, whose crest was stamped upon a quantity of plate he had brought with him to California. The plate, together with an exceptionally good cook, which he had also brought, and his own epicurean tastes, he utilized in the usual practical Californian fashion by starting a rather expensive half-club, half-restaurant in the lower part of the building—which he ruled somewhat autocratically, as became his crest. The restaurant was too expensive for me to patronize, but I saw many of its frequenters as well as those who had rooms at the club. They were men of very distinct personality; a few celebrated, and nearly all notorious. They represented a Bohemianism—if such it could be called—less innocent than my later experiences. I remember, however, one handsome young fellow whom I used to meet occasionally on the staircase, who captured my youthful fancy. I met him only at midday, as he did not rise till late, and this fact, with a certain scrupulous elegance and neatness in his dress, ought to have made me suspect that he was a gambler. In my inexperience it only invested him with a certain romantic mystery.

One morning as I was going out to my very early breakfast at a cheap Italian cafe on Long Wharf, I was surprised to find him also descending the staircase. He was scrupulously dressed even at that early hour, but I was struck by the fact that he was all in black, and his slight figure, buttoned to the throat in a tightly fitting frock coat, gave, I fancied, a singular melancholy to his pale Southern face. Nevertheless, he greeted me with more than his usual serene cordiality, and I remembered that he looked up with a half-puzzled, half-amused expression at the rosy morning sky as he walked a few steps with me down the deserted street. I could not help saying that I was astonished to see him up so early, and he admitted that it was a break in his usual habits, but added with a smiling significance I afterwards remembered that it was "an even chance if he did it again." As we neared the street corner a man in a buggy drove up impatiently. In spite of the driver's evident haste, my handsome acquaintance got in leisurely, and, lifting his glossy hat to me with a pleasant smile, was driven away. I have a very lasting recollection of his face and figure as the buggy disappeared down the empty street. I never saw him again. It was not until a week later that I knew that an hour after he left me that morning he was lying dead in a little hollow behind the Mission Dolores— shot through the heart in a duel for which he had risen so early.

I recall another incident of that period, equally characteristic, but happily less tragic in sequel. I was in the restaurant one morning talking to my cousin when a man entered hastily and said something to him in a hurried whisper. My cousin contracted his eyebrows and uttered a suppressed oath. Then with a gesture of warning to the man he crossed the room quietly to a table where a regular habitue of the restaurant was lazily finishing his breakfast. A large silver coffee-pot with a stiff wooden handle stood on the table before him. My cousin leaned over the guest familiarly and apparently made some hospitable inquiry as to his wants, with his hand resting lightly on the coffee-pot handle. Then—possibly because, my curiosity having been excited, I was watching him more intently than the others—I saw what probably no one else saw—that he deliberately upset the coffee-pot and its contents over the guest's shirt and waistcoat. As the victim sprang up with an exclamation, my cousin overwhelmed him with apologies for his carelessness, and, with protestations of sorrow for the accident, actually insisted upon dragging the man upstairs into his own private room, where he furnished him with a shirt and waistcoat of his own. The side door had scarcely closed upon them, and I was still lost in wonder at what I had seen, when a man entered from the street. He was one of the desperate set I have already spoken of, and thoroughly well known to those present. He cast a glance around the room, nodded to one or two of the guests, and then walked to a side table and took up a newspaper. I was conscious at once that a singular constraint had come over the other guests—a nervous awkwardness that at last seemed to make itself known to the man himself, who, after an affected yawn or two, laid down the paper and walked out.

"That was a mighty close call," said one of the guests with a sigh of relief.

"You bet! And that coffee-pot spill was the luckiest kind of accident for Peters," returned another.

"For both," added the first speaker, "for Peters was armed too, and would have seen him come in!"

A word or two explained all. Peters and the last comer had quarreled a day or two before, and had separated with the intention to "shoot on sight," that is, wherever they met,—a form of duel common to those days. The accidental meeting in the restaurant would have been the occasion, with the usual sanguinary consequence, but for the word of warning given to my cousin by a passer-by who knew that Peters' antagonist was coming to the restaurant to look at the papers. Had my cousin repeated the warning to Peters himself he would only have prepared him for the conflict—which he would not have shirked—and so precipitated the affray.

The ruse of upsetting the coffee-pot, which everybody but myself thought an accident, was to get him out of the room before the other entered. I was too young then to venture to intrude upon my cousin's secrets, but two or three years afterwards I taxed him with the trick and he admitted it regretfully. I believe that a strict interpretation of the "code" would have condemned his act as unsportsmanlike, if not UNFAIR!

I recall another incident connected with the building equally characteristic of the period. The United States Branch Mint stood very near it, and its tall, factory-like chimneys overshadowed my cousin's roof. Some scandal had arisen from an alleged leakage of gold in the manipulation of that metal during the various processes of smelting and refining. One of the excuses offered was the volatilization of the precious metal and its escape through the draft of the tall chimneys. All San Francisco laughed at this explanation until it learned that a corroboration of the theory had been established by an assay of the dust and grime of the roofs in the vicinity of the Mint. These had yielded distinct traces of gold. San Francisco stopped laughing, and that portion of it which had roofs in the neighborhood at once began prospecting. Claims were staked out on these airy placers, and my cousin's roof, being the very next one to the chimney, and presumably "in the lead," was disposed of to a speculative company for a considerable sum. I remember my cousin telling me the story—for the occurrence was quite recent—and taking me with him to the roof to explain it, but I am afraid I was more attracted by the mystery of the closely guarded building, and the strangely tinted smoke which arose from this temple where money was actually being "made," than by anything else. Nor did I dream as I stood there—a very lanky, open-mouthed youth—that only three or four years later I should be the secretary of its superintendent. In my more adventurous ambition I am afraid I would have accepted the suggestion half-heartedly. Merely to have helped to stamp the gold which other people had adventurously found was by no means a part of my youthful dreams.

At the time of these earlier impressions the Chinese had not yet become the recognized factors in the domestic and business economy of the city which they had come to be when I returned from the mines three years later. Yet they were even then a more remarkable and picturesque contrast to the bustling, breathless, and brand-new life of San Francisco than the Spaniard. The latter seldom flaunted his faded dignity in the principal thoroughfares. "John" was to be met everywhere. It was a common thing to see a long file of sampan coolies carrying their baskets slung between them, on poles, jostling a modern, well-dressed crowd in Montgomery Street, or to get a whiff of their burned punk in the side streets; while the road leading to their temporary burial-ground at Lone Mountain was littered with slips of colored paper scattered from their funerals. They brought an atmosphere of the Arabian Nights into the hard, modern civilization; their shops—not always confined at that time to a Chinese quarter—were replicas of the bazaars of Canton and Peking, with their quaint display of little dishes on which tidbits of food delicacies were exposed for sale, all of the dimensions and unreality of a doll's kitchen or a child's housekeeping.

They were a revelation to the Eastern immigrant, whose preconceived ideas of them were borrowed from the ballet or pantomime; they did not wear scalloped drawers and hats with jingling bells on their points, nor did I ever see them dance with their forefingers vertically extended. They were always neatly dressed, even the commonest of coolies, and their festive dresses were marvels. As traders they were grave and patient; as servants they were sad and civil, and all were singularly infantine in their natural simplicity. The living representatives of the oldest civilization in the world, they seemed like children. Yet they kept their beliefs and sympathies to themselves, never fraternizing with the fanqui, or foreign devil, or losing their singular racial qualities. They indulged in their own peculiar habits; of their social and inner life, San Francisco knew but little and cared less. Even at this early period, and before I came to know them more intimately, I remember an incident of their daring fidelity to their own customs that was accidentally revealed to me. I had become acquainted with a Chinese youth of about my own age, as I imagined,—although from mere outward appearance it was generally impossible to judge of a Chinaman's age between the limits of seventeen and forty years,—and he had, in a burst of confidence, taken me to see some characteristic sights in a Chinese warehouse within a stone's throw of the Plaza. I was struck by the singular circumstance that while the warehouse was an erection of wood in the ordinary hasty Californian style, there were certain brick and stone divisions in its interior, like small rooms or closets, evidently added by the Chinamen tenants. My companion stopped before a long, very narrow entrance, a mere longitudinal slit in the brick wall, and with a wink of infantine deviltry motioned me to look inside. I did so, and saw a room, really a cell, of fair height but scarcely six feet square, and barely able to contain a rude, slanting couch of stone covered with matting, on which lay, at a painful angle, a richly dressed Chinaman. A single glance at his dull, staring, abstracted eyes and half-opened mouth showed me he was in an opium trance. This was not in itself a novel sight, and I was moving away when I was suddenly startled by the appearance of his hands, which were stretched helplessly before him on his body, and at first sight seemed to be in a kind of wicker cage.

I then saw that his finger-nails were seven or eight inches long, and were supported by bamboo splints. Indeed, they were no longer human nails, but twisted and distorted quills, giving him the appearance of having gigantic claws. "Velly big Chinaman," whispered my cheerful friend; "first-chop man—high classee—no can washee—no can eat—no dlinke, no catchee him own glub allee same nothee man—China boy must catchee glub for him, allee time! Oh, him first-chop man—you bettee!"

Bret Harte

I had heard of this singular custom of indicating caste before, and was amazed and disgusted, but I was not prepared for what followed. My companion, evidently thinking he had impressed me, grew more reckless as showman, and saying to me, "Now me showee you one funny thing—heap makee you laugh," led me hurriedly across a little courtyard swarming with chickens and rabbits, when he stopped before another inclosure. Suddenly brushing past an astonished Chinaman who seemed to be standing guard, he thrust me into the inclosure in front of a most extraordinary object. It was a Chinaman, wearing a huge, square, wooden frame fastened around his neck like a collar, and fitting so tightly and rigidly that the flesh rose in puffy weals around his cheeks. He was chained to a post, although it was as impossible for him to have escaped with his wooden cage through the narrow doorway as it was for him to lie down and rest in it. Yet I am bound to say that his eyes and face expressed nothing but apathy, and there was no appeal to the sympathy of the stranger. My companion said hurriedly,—

"Velly bad man; stealee heap from Chinamen," and then, apparently alarmed at his own indiscreet intrusion, hustled me away as quickly as possible amid a shrill cackling of protestation from a few of his own countrymen who had joined the one who was keeping guard. In another moment we were in the street again—scarce a step from the Plaza, in the full light of Western civilization—not a stone's throw from the courts of justice.

My companion took to his heels and left me standing there bewildered and indignant. I could not rest until I had told my story, but without betraying my companion, to an elder acquaintance, who laid the facts before the police authorities. I had expected to be closely cross-examined—to be doubted—to be disbelieved. To my surprise, I was told that the police had already cognizance of similar cases of illegal and barbarous punishments, but that the victims themselves refused to testify against their countrymen—and it was impossible to convict or even to identify them. "A white man can't tell one Chinese from another, and there are always a dozen of 'em ready to swear that the man you've got isn't the one." I was startled to reflect that I, too, could not have conscientiously sworn to either jailor or the tortured prisoner—or perhaps even to my cheerful companion. The police, on some pretext, made a raid upon the premises a day or two afterwards, but without result. I wondered if they had caught sight of the high-class, first-chop individual, with the helplessly outstretched fingers, as that story I had kept to myself.

But these barbaric vestiges in John Chinaman's habits did not affect his relations with the San Franciscans. He was singularly peaceful, docile, and harmless as a servant, and, with rare exceptions, honest and temperate. If he sometimes matched cunning with cunning, it was the flattery of imitation. He did most of the menial work of San Francisco, and did it cleanly. Except that he exhaled a peculiar druglike odor, he was not personally offensive in domestic contact, and by virtue of being the recognized laundryman of the whole community his own blouses were always freshly washed and ironed. His conversational reserve arose, not from his having to deal with an unfamiliar language,—for he had picked up a picturesque and varied vocabulary with ease,—but from his natural temperament. He was devoid of curiosity, and utterly unimpressed by anything but the purely business concerns of those he served. Domestic secrets were safe with him; his indifference to your thoughts, actions, and feelings had all the contempt which his three thousand years of history and his innate belief in your inferiority seemed to justify. He was blind and deaf in your household because you didn't interest him in the least. It was said that a gentleman, who wished to test his impassiveness, arranged with his wife to come home one day and, in the hearing of his Chinese waiter who was more than usually intelligent—to disclose with well-simulated emotion the details of a murder he had just committed. He did so. The Chinaman heard it without a sign of horror or attention even to the lifting of an eyelid, but continued his duties unconcerned. Unfortunately, the gentleman, in order to increase the horror of the situation, added that now there was nothing left for him but to cut his throat. At this John quietly left the room. The gentleman was delighted at the success of his ruse until the door reopened and John reappeared with his master's razor, which he quietly slipped—as if it had been a forgotten fork—beside his master's plate, and calmly resumed his serving. I have always considered this story to be quite as improbable as it was inartistic, from its tacit admission of a certain interest on the part of the Chinaman. I never knew one who would have been sufficiently concerned to go for the razor.

His taciturnity and reticence may have been confounded with rudeness of address, although he was always civil enough. "I see you have listened to me and done exactly what I told you," said a lady, commending some performance of her servant after a previous lengthy lecture; "that's very nice." "Yes," said John calmly, "you talkee allee time; talkee allee too much." "I always find Ling very polite," said another lady, speaking of her cook, "but I wish he did not always say to me, 'Goodnight, John,' in a high falsetto voice." She had not recognized the fact that he was simply repeating her own salutation with his marvelous instinct of relentless imitation, even as to voice. I hesitate to record the endless stories of his misapplication of that faculty which were then current, from the one of the laundryman who removed the buttons from the shirts that were sent to him to wash that they might agree with the condition of the one offered him as a pattern for "doing up," to that of the unfortunate employer who, while showing John how to handle valuable china carefully, had the misfortune to drop a plate himself—an accident which was followed by the prompt breaking of another by the neophyte, with the addition of "Oh, hellee!" in humble imitation of his master.

I have spoken of his general cleanliness; I am reminded of one or two exceptions, which I think, however, were errors of zeal. His manner of sprinkling clothes in preparing them for ironing was peculiar. He would fill his mouth with perfectly pure water from a glass beside him, and then, by one dexterous movement of his lips in a prolonged expiration, squirt the water in an almost invisible misty shower on the article before him. Shocking as this was at first to the sensibilities of many American employers, it was finally accepted, and even commended. It was some time after this that the mistress of a household, admiring the deft way in which her cook had spread a white sauce on certain dishes, was cheerfully informed that the method was "allee same."

His recreations at that time were chiefly gambling, for the Chinese theatre wherein the latter produced his plays (which lasted for several months and comprised the events of a whole dynasty) was not yet built. But he had one or two companies of jugglers who occasionally performed also at American theatres. I remember a singular incident which attended the debut of a newly arrived company. It seemed that the company had been taken on their Chinese reputation solely, and there had been no previous rehearsal before the American stage manager. The theatre was filled with an audience of decorous and respectable San Franciscans of both sexes. It was suddenly emptied in the middle of the performance; the curtain came down with an alarmed and blushing manager apologizing to deserted benches, and the show abruptly terminated. Exactly WHAT had happened

Bret Harte

never appeared in the public papers, nor in the published apology of the manager. It afforded a few days' mirth for wicked San Francisco, and it was epigrammatically summed up in the remark that "no woman could be found in San Francisco who was at that performance, and no man who was not." Yet it was alleged even by John's worst detractors that he was innocent of any intended offense. Equally innocent, but perhaps more morally instructive, was an incident that brought his career as a singularly successful physician to a disastrous close. An ordinary native Chinese doctor, practicing entirely among his own countrymen, was reputed to have made extraordinary cures with two or three American patients. With no other advertising than this, and apparently no other inducement offered to the public than what their curiosity suggested, he was presently besieged by hopeful and eager sufferers. Hundreds of patients were turned away from his crowded doors. Two interpreters sat, day and night, translating the ills of ailing San Francisco to this medical oracle, and dispensing his prescriptions— usually small powders—in exchange for current coin. In vain the regular practitioners pointed out that the Chinese possessed no superior medical knowledge, and that their religion, which proscribed dissection and autopsies, naturally limited their understanding of the body into which they put their drugs. Finally they prevailed upon an eminent Chinese authority to give them a list of the remedies generally used in the Chinese pharmacopoeia, and this was privately circulated. For obvious reasons I may not repeat it here. But it was summed up—again after the usual Californian epigrammatic style—by the remark that "whatever were the comparative merits of Chinese and American practice, a simple perusal of the list would prove that the Chinese were capable of producing the most powerful emetic known." The craze subsided in a single day; the interpreters and their oracle vanished; the Chinese doctors' signs, which had multiplied, disappeared, and San Francisco awoke cured of its madness, at the cost of some thousand dollars.

My Bohemian wanderings were confined to the limits of the city, for the very good reason that there was little elsewhere to go. San Francisco was then bounded on one side by the monotonously restless waters of the bay, and on the other by a stretch of equally restless and monotonously shifting sand dunes as far as the Pacific shore. Two roads penetrated this waste: one to Lone Mountain—the cemetery; the other to the Cliff House—happily described as "an eight-mile drive with a cocktail at the end of it." Nor was the humor entirely confined to this felicitous description. The Cliff House itself, half restaurant, half drinking saloon, fronting the ocean and the Seal Rock, where disporting seals were the chief object of interest, had its own peculiar symbol. The decanters, wine-glasses, and tumblers at the bar were all engraved in old English script with the legal initials "L. S." (Locus Sigilli),—"the place of the seal."

On the other hand, Lone Mountain, a dreary promontory giving upon the Golden Gate and its striking sunsets, had little to soften its weird suggestiveness. As the common goal of the successful and unsuccessful, the carved and lettered shaft of the man who had made a name, and the staring blank headboard of the man who had none, climbed the sandy slopes together. I have seen the funerals of the respectable citizen who had died peacefully in his bed, and the notorious desperado who had died "with his boots on," followed by an equally impressive cortege of sorrowing friends, and often the self-same priest. But more awful than its barren loneliness was the utter absence of peacefulness and rest in this dismal promontory. By some wicked irony of its situation and climate it was the personification of unrest and change. The incessant trade winds carried its loose sands hither and thither, uncovering the decaying coffins of early pioneers, to bury the wreaths and flowers, laid on a grave of to-day, under their obliterating waves. No tree to shade them from the glaring sky above could live in those winds, no turf would lie there to resist the encroaching sand below. The dead were harried and hustled even in their graves by the persistent sun, the unremitting wind, and the unceasing sea. The departing mourner saw the contour of the very mountain itself change with the shifting dunes as he passed, and his last look beyond rested on the hurrying, eager waves forever hastening to the Golden Gate.

If I were asked to say what one thing impressed me as the dominant and characteristic note of San Francisco, I should say it was this untiring presence of sun and wind and sea. They typified, even if they were not, as I sometimes fancied, the actual incentive to the fierce, restless life of the city. I could not think of San Francisco without the trade winds; I could not imagine its strange, incongruous, multigenerous procession marching to any other music. They were always there in my youthful recollections; they were there in my more youthful dreams of the past as the mysterious vientes generales that blew the Philippine galleons home.

For six months they blew from the northwest, for six months from the southwest, with unvarying persistency. They were there every morning, glittering in the equally persistent sunlight, to chase the San Franciscan from his slumber; they were there at midday, to stir his pulses with their beat; they were there again at night, to hurry him through the bleak and flaring gas-lit streets to bed. They left their mark on every windward street or fence or gable, on the outlying sand dunes; they lashed the slow coasters home, and hurried them to sea again; they whipped the bay into turbulence on their way to Contra Costa, whose level shoreland oaks they had trimmed to windward as cleanly and sharply as with a pruning-shears. Untiring themselves, they allowed no laggards; they drove the San Franciscan from the wall against which he would have leaned, from the scant shade in which at noontide he might have rested. They turned his smallest fires into conflagrations, and kept him ever alert, watchful, and eager. In return, they scavenged his city and held it clean and wholesome; in summer they brought him the soft sea-fog for a few hours to soothe his abraded surfaces; in winter they brought the rains and dashed the whole coast-line with flowers, and the staring sky above it with soft, unwonted clouds. They were always there—strong, vigilant, relentless, material, unyielding, triumphant.

ABOUT THE AUTHOR

 **Francis Bret Harte** (August 25, 1836–May 6, 1902) was an American author and poet, best remembered for his accounts of pioneering life in California.

Born in Albany, New York, Harte moved to California in 1853, later working there in a number of capacities, including miner, teacher, messenger, and journalist. He spent part of his life in the northern California coast town now known as Arcata, at the time it was just a mining camp on Humboldt Bay.

His first literary efforts, including poetry and prose, appeared in The Californian, an early literary journal edited by Charles Henry Webb. In 1868 he became editor of The Overland Monthly, another new literary magazine, but this one more in tune with the pioneering spirit of excitement in California. His story, "The Luck of Roaring Camp," appeared in the magazine's second edition, propelling Harte to nationwide fame.

As an established literary figure, he was appointed to the position of United States Consul in the town of Krefeld, Germany in 1878 and Glasgow in 1880. In 1885 he settled in London. During the thirty years he spent in Europe, he never abandoned writing, and maintained a prodigious output of stories that retained the freshness of his earlier work. He died in England in 1902.

Other books by this author

Openings in the Old Trail
Sally Dows and Other Stories
Stories in Light and Shadow
Tales of the Argonauts
Tales of Trail and Town
The Three Partners
Maruja
By Shore and Sedge
Colonel Starbottle's Client and Other Stories
Clarence
Cressy
Devil's Ford
Frontier Stories
In a Hollow of the Hills
In the Carquinez Woods
Jeff Briggs's Love Story
Snow-Bound at Eagle's
The Argonauts of North Liberty
The Bell-Ringer of Angel's and Other Stories
The Crusade of the Excelsior
The Story of a Mine

Choose from Thousands of 1stWorldLibrary Classics By

A. M. Barnard
Ada Leverson
Adolphus William Ward
Aesop
Agatha Christie
Alexander Aaronsohn
Alexander Kielland
Alexandre Dumas
Alfred Gatty
Alfred Ollivant
Alice Duer Miller
Alice Turner Curtis
Alice Dunbar
Allen Chapman
Alleyne Ireland
Ambrose Bierce
Amelia E. Barr
Amory H. Bradford
Andrew Lang
Andrew McFarland Davis
Andy Adams
Angela Brazil
Anna Alice Chapin
Anna Sewell
Annie Besant
Annie Hamilton Donnell
Annie Payson Call
Annie Roe Carr
Annonaymous
Anton Chekhov
Archibald Lee Fletcher
Arnold Bennett
Arthur C. Benson
Arthur Conan Doyle
Arthur M. Winfield
Arthur Ransome
Arthur Schnitzler
Arthur Train
Atticus
B.H. Baden-Powell
B. M. Bower
B. C. Chatterjee
Baroness Emmuska Orczy
Baroness Orczy
Basil King
Bayard Taylor
Ben Macomber
Bertha Muzzy Bower
Bjornstjerne Bjornson

Booth Tarkington
Boyd Cable
Bram Stoker
C. Collodi
C. E. Orr
C. M. Ingleby
Carolyn Wells
Catherine Parr Traill
Charles A. Eastman
Charles Amory Beach
Charles Dickens
Charles Dudley Warner
Charles Farrar Browne
Charles Ives
Charles Kingsley
Charles Klein
Charles Hanson Towne
Charles Lathrop Pack
Charles Romyn Dake
Charles Whibley
Charles Willing Beale
Charlotte M. Braeme
Charlotte M. Yonge
Charlotte Perkins Stetson
Clair W. Hayes
Clarence Day Jr.
Clarence E. Mulford
Clemence Housman
Confucius
Coningsby Dawson
Cornelis DeWitt Wilcox
Cyril Burleigh
D. H. Lawrence
Daniel Defoe
David Garnett
Dinah Craik
Don Carlos Janes
Donald Keyhoe
Dorothy Kilner
Dougan Clark
Douglas Fairbanks
E. Nesbit
E. P. Roe
E. Phillips Oppenheim
E. S. Brooks
Earl Barnes
Edgar Rice Burroughs
Edith Van Dyne
Edith Wharton

Edward Everett Hale
Edward J. O'Biren
Edward S. Ellis
Edwin L. Arnold
Eleanor Atkins
Eleanor Hallowell Abbott
Eliot Gregory
Elizabeth Gaskell
Elizabeth McCracken
Elizabeth Von Arnim
Ellem Key
Emerson Hough
Emilie F. Carlen
Emily Bronte
Emily Dickinson
Enid Bagnold
Enilor Macartney Lane
Erasmus W. Jones
Ernie Howard Pie
Ethel May Dell
Ethel Turner
Ethel Watts Mumford
Eugene Sue
Eugenie Foa
Eugene Wood
Eustace Hale Ball
Evelyn Everett-green
Everard Cotes
F. H. Cheley
F. J. Cross
F. Marion Crawford
Fannie E. Newberry
Federick Austin Ogg
Ferdinand Ossendowski
Fergus Hume
Florence A. Kilpatrick
Fremont B. Deering
Francis Bacon
Francis Darwin
Frances Hodgson Burnett
Frances Parkinson Keyes
Frank Gee Patchin
Frank Harris
Frank Jewett Mather
Frank L. Packard
Frank V. Webster
Frederic Stewart Isham
Frederick Trevor Hill
Frederick Winslow Taylor

Friedrich Kerst
Friedrich Nietzsche
Fyodor Dostoyevsky
G.A. Henty
G.K. Chesterton
Gabrielle E. Jackson
Garrett P. Serviss
Gaston Leroux
George A. Warren
George Ade
Geroge Bernard Shaw
George Cary Eggleston
George Durston
George Ebers
George Eliot
George Gissing
George MacDonald
George Meredith
George Orwell
George Sylvester Viereck
George Tucker
George W. Cable
George Wharton James
Gertrude Atherton
Gordon Casserly
Grace E. King
Grace Gallatin
Grace Greenwood
Grant Allen
Guillermo A. Sherwell
Gulielma Zollinger
Gustav Flaubert
H. A. Cody
H. B. Irving
H. C. Bailey
H. G. Wells
H. H. Munro
H. Irving Hancock
H. R. Naylor
H. Rider Haggard
H. W. C. Davis
Haldeman Julius
Hall Caine
Hamilton Wright Mabie
Hans Christian Andersen
Harold Avery
Harold McGrath
Harriet Beecher Stowe
Harry Castlemon
Harry Coghill
Harry Houidini

Hayden Carruth
Helent Hunt Jackson
Helen Nicolay
Hendrik Conscience
Hendy David Thoreau
Henri Barbusse
Henrik Ibsen
Henry Adams
Henry Ford
Henry Frost
Henry James
Henry Jones Ford
Henry Seton Merriman
Henry W Longfellow
Herbert A. Giles
Herbert Carter
Herbert N. Casson
Herman Hesse
Hildegard G. Frey
Homer
Honore De Balzac
Horace B. Day
Horace Walpole
Horatio Alger Jr.
Howard Pyle
Howard R. Garis
Hugh Lofting
Hugh Walpole
Humphry Ward
Ian Maclaren
Inez Haynes Gillmore
Irving Bacheller
Isabel Cecilia Williams
Isabel Hornibrook
Israel Abrahams
Ivan Turgenev
J. G.Austin
J. Henri Fabre
J. M. Barrie
J. M. Walsh
J. Macdonald Oxley
J. R. Miller
J. S. Fletcher
J. S. Knowles
J. Storer Clouston
J. W. Duffield
Jack London
Jacob Abbott
James Allen
James Andrews
James Baldwin

James Branch Cabell
James DeMille
James Joyce
James Lane Allen
James Lane Allen
James Oliver Curwood
James Oppenheim
James Otis
James R. Driscoll
Jane Abbott
Jane Austen
Jane L. Stewart
Janet Aldridge
Jens Peter Jacobsen
Jerome K. Jerome
Jessie Graham Flower
John Buchan
John Burroughs
John Cournos
John F. Kennedy
John Gay
John Glasworthy
John Habberton
John Joy Bell
John Kendrick Bangs
John Milton
John Philip Sousa
John Taintor Foote
Jonas Lauritz Idemil Lie
Jonathan Swift
Joseph A. Altsheler
Joseph Carey
Joseph Conrad
Joseph E. Badger Jr
Joseph Hergesheimer
Joseph Jacobs
Jules Vernes
Julian Hawthrone
Julie A Lippmann
Justin Huntly McCarthy
Kakuzo Okakura
Karle Wilson Baker
Kate Chopin
Kenneth Grahame
Kenneth McGaffey
Kate Langley Bosher
Kate Langley Bosher
Katherine Cecil Thurston
Katherine Stokes
L. A. Abbot
L. T. Meade

L. Frank Baum
Latta Griswold
Laura Dent Crane
Laura Lee Hope
Laurence Housman
Lawrence Beasley
Leo Tolstoy
Leonid Andreyev
Lewis Carroll
Lewis Sperry Chafer
Lilian Bell
Lloyd Osbourne
Louis Hughes
Louis Joseph Vance
Louis Tracy
Louisa May Alcott
Lucy Fitch Perkins
Lucy Maud Montgomery
Luther Benson
Lydia Miller Middleton
Lyndon Orr
M. Corvus
M. H. Adams
Margaret E. Sangster
Margret Howth
Margaret Vandercook
Margaret W. Hungerford
Margret Penrose
Maria Edgeworth
Maria Thompson Daviess
Mariano Azuela
Marion Polk Angellotti
Mark Overton
Mark Twain
Mary Austin
Mary Catherine Crowley
Mary Cole
Mary Hastings Bradley
Mary Roberts Rinehart
Mary Rowlandson
M. Wollstonecraft Shelley
Maud Lindsay
Max Beerbohm
Myra Kelly
Nathaniel Hawthrone
Nicolo Machiavelli
O. F. Walton
Oscar Wilde

Owen Johnson
P.G. Wodehouse
Paul and Mabel Thorne
Paul G. Tomlinson
Paul Severing
Percy Brebner
Percy Keese Fitzhugh
Peter B. Kyne
Plato
Quincy Allen
R. Derby Holmes
R. L. Stevenson
R. S. Ball
Rabindranath Tagore
Rahul Alvares
Ralph Bonehill
Ralph Henry Barbour
Ralph Victor
Ralph Waldo Emmerson
Rene Descartes
Ray Cummings
Rex Beach
Rex E. Beach
Richard Harding Davis
Richard Jefferies
Richard Le Gallienne
Robert Barr
Robert Frost
Robert Gordon Anderson
Robert L. Drake
Robert Lansing
Robert Lynd
Robert Michael Ballantyne
Robert W. Chambers
Rosa Nouchette Carey
Rudyard Kipling
Saint Augustine
Samuel B. Allison
Samuel Hopkins Adams
Sarah Bernhardt
Sarah C. Hallowell
Selma Lagerlof
Sherwood Anderson
Sigmund Freud
Standish O'Grady
Stanley Weyman
Stella Benson
Stella M. Francis

Stephen Crane
Stewart Edward White
Stijn Streuvels
Swami Abhedananda
Swami Parmananda
T. S. Ackland
T. S. Arthur
The Princess Der Ling
Thomas A. Janvier
Thomas A Kempis
Thomas Anderton
Thomas Bailey Aldrich
Thomas Bulfinch
Thomas De Quincey
Thomas Dixon
Thomas H. Huxley
Thomas Hardy
Thomas More
Thornton W. Burgess
U. S. Grant
Upton Sinclair
Valentine Williams
Various Authors
Vaughan Kester
Victor Appleton
Victor G. Durham
Victoria Cross
Virginia Woolf
Wadsworth Camp
Walter Camp
Walter Scott
Washington Irving
Wilbur Lawton
Wilkie Collins
Willa Cather
Willard F. Baker
William Dean Howells
William le Queux
W. Makepeace Thackeray
William W. Walter
William Shakespeare
Winston Churchill
Yei Theodora Ozaki
Yogi Ramacharaka
Young E. Allison
Zane Grey

www.ingramcontent.com/pod-product-compliance
Lightning Source LLC
Chambersburg PA
CBHW020205270626
47157CB00028B/1414